THE
STUL

THE
STUDENT

IAIN RYAN

echo

echo

A division of Bonnier Publishing Australia
534 Church Street, Richmond
Victoria Australia 3121
www.echopublishing.com.au

First published 2017

Printed in Australia at Griffin Press.
Only wood grown from sustainable regrowth forests is used in the manufacture of paper found in this book.

Cover design by Alissa Dinallo
Cover image: Shutterstock
Page design and typesetting by Shaun Jury
Typeset in Fairfield

National Library of Australia Cataloguing-in-Publication entry:
    Creator: Ryan Iain, author.
    Title: The Student / Iain Ryan.
    ISBN: 9781760406370 (paperback)
    ISBN: 9781760408381 (ebook)
    ISBN: 9781760408398 (mobi)
    Subjects: Marijuana abuse—Fiction. Drug abuse—Fiction.
    Gatton (Qld.)—Fiction.

 @bonnierau
@bonnierpublishingau
@bonnierpublishingau

For Iris,
Forever

To philosophise with open eyes is to philosophise in the dark. Only the blind can look straight at the sun.

– Louis Althusser

WEDNESDAY

The white sun in my eyes. A road train sprays gravel at the phone booth like a bomb blast. It's September and September is the month my supply goes bad. An early end to winter. A giant mess.

I shout into the phone:

'– All I have is grief. There hasn't been bud in a fortnight.'

'– I don't do that. Jesse looks after it.'

'– No one's seen him.'

My beeper goes off. A landline. I know the number. *Iris.*

'– I don't give a fuck.'

'– Okay, well, take your chances with them, then.'

I slam the phone back into the cradle and put my head against the glass. Another truck, another blast. The booth rumbles and fills with dust. A white piece of paper flaps at my feet, caught under the door. I reach down and pick it up.

Missing: Maya Kibby

There's the photo from her student card. This flyer is a month old. She's no longer missing. They found her body out in the scrub a week ago. Maya was the first person I knew who was murdered.

Gatton, 1994.

* * *

Iris answers the phone like she hasn't paged me:

'Oh right. Is Jesse at yours?' she says.

'No.'

No one has seen Jesse.

She sighs. Jesse and Iris broke up a few weeks back. I introduced them. Jesse, my supplier, my friend. Jesse, Iris's ex-boyfriend. This is student life in Gatton. 'Heard he was heading out of town,' she says. 'But I just wanted to make sure he isn't with you.'

Jesse's like this. He disappears. But he never stays at my place. No one ever stays at my place.

I scratch at my scalp and say, 'What's up with you?'

'What do you mean?'

I stare out at the road. Things are weird between us at the moment. 'I don't know,' I say, a lie. 'Are you holding? I'm totally, totally out.'

'Just my own stash.'

'Fuck. *Fuck*.'

'You need money, Nate?'

'No. I need my supply, then I need money. Oh, man. This better not be like last time.'

'You need to get yourself loose of him,' Iris says. She's in her kitchen, I can tell. She's moving something metallic around in the sink.

'I can't. I don't have enough.'

'How much is enough, then?'

The line goes dead.

I have piles of money out. A valley of hundreds, a hill of blue tens, a summit of fives. Plastic money, half of it greasy with who-knows-what. There's a shopping bag of pot leaf beside me on the bench seat, down by my thigh. I'm too scared to have it up on the kitchenette table. Even shit weed is scarce at the moment.

I'm light.
I'm fucked.
So many layers of fucked. So many layers.

Graham – who owns my caravan and manages the park –
he has me here because he needs a weed connection. He doesn't need another tenant. He tells me that the park is a nightmare *because* of the tenants. He gave me a fortnight to cough up his dope. *Weed or leave.* That was a week ago.

Graham's not alone in his ire. All my customers are bugging out. They're all getting the first inkling of a weed drought and they're all hitting my beeper, as if calling me twice a day is going to change something.

And then there's my family. My mother lost her mind a couple of years ago and now my dad is unemployed. He got fired from his gig as a school groundskeeper because he kept taking carer's leave. Some days, Mum is so bad he can't leave her alone in a room. And the weird thing about Dad is that he can't accept that this thing with her is costing money. They're months over on the mortgage. The *second* mortgage. So we need to magically produce thirty-six thousand by the end of the year – on top of the current repayments – just to keep the house I grew up in.

I send them money. Dad says the same thing every time: *Thank god for McDonald's,* and *Son, we'll pay you back one day,* and I thank god too, every time. I thank god that Dad never studied business because then he'd know that a line cook at the Gatton McDonald's could never – not in a million years – make the cash I'm sending home.

Except, this week, I'm not sending anything. That plan is disappearing before my eyes.

Because I'm light.
Getting lighter.
Shedding customers.

Eviction pending.
Plans going down the toilet.
Because of Jesse.
I figure I'm a week away from real trouble.

D ark out through the windows:
      '– Nah, it's round the other side. Jesus.'

'All them other vans face that way, I just reckoned...'

'What? Goddamnit, keep your voice down.'

They sound big. One of them finds the door to my caravan.

It's locked but the whole thing is so old and rusted that the lock doesn't mean much.

I sit up and grab the hammer I keep by the bed.

There's a sound: a key sliding in.

I watch in horror as the door swings open.

The whole caravan creaks and shifts when the first one steps up. In the dark, he looks like a bear wearing a human head. A long black beard, dark vest, hair trailing over his shoulders.

The other one follows. He's smaller. Shorter hair. Same beard. Same vest.

Bikies.

'Hello?' says one of them.

The lights come on.

My eyes burn. I focus and find them both standing there smiling at me.

'This is a new one,' says the bear. 'Sleeps with a hammer.'

I can see now that the smaller one's holding a rifle. It's not aimed at me. He's just holding it.

'Don't fucking hit me with that thing,' says the bear. He comes and sits on the edge of the bed. The bed almost collapses under the weight of him. 'Got anything to drink, kid? I know you're out of weed because we just bought a key to your place with a fifty bag.'

He dangles the key from his hand.

Fucking Graham.

I throw the hammer on the floor.

Their names are Dennis and Hatch and my caravan looks crowded with them in it. Dennis is the bear. Hatch is the one with the rifle. He stands it against the kitchen counter as I check the van's little fridge. I have three bottles of a neighbour's home brew and a half-empty goon bag of red wine. Dennis peers in over my shoulder. He grunts when I pull out the beer. The two of them push themselves into the van's breakfast nook.

'Sit down, kid.'

I stay by the fridge.

Dennis says, 'You seen Jesse?'

'No.'

'You know where Jesse is?'

'I don't know.'

'That's a pity.'

I wait. They look at each other, take a mouthful of beer each.

'I just sell for him,' I say.

'We know who you are,' says Hatch.

'You're Jesse's partner. One of 'em anyhow,' adds Dennis.

'That's not... There's no... We're not partners. He's more like a supplier.'

'Well, then I guess that makes you my bitch then, because I'm Jesse's *supplier*,' says Dennis. He waves his hand. 'I said come 'ere. Sit.'

I do it, squeezing into the tiny breakfast nook beside Dennis. As soon as I'm settled, Dennis grabs me by the back of the scalp and slams my head down into the Formica table. The pain is instant yet somehow his grip on my hair is worse, the skin on my face pinched back. He grinds my head down into the tabletop.

Hatch leans over to my ear and whispers, 'The way we see it. You go and find Jesse or you cover his debts.' Hatch slaps the table by my face. 'That was a question, arsehole.'

Dennis lets me up. 'You got forty-five grand? You got that on you?'

'No. I'm waiting on –'

Dennis shoves me out onto the van floor. I slide across the lino until my head connects with the wood panel of the cupboard under the sink.

For a sickly moment, everything stops:

The rifle.

It's right there.

We all stare at it.

Dennis sighs.

Hatch says, 'Well, you're the idiot that threw him that way.'

'I'm not going to touch that,' I say. I don't know what's happening.

Dennis sighs again, louder. 'Fuck.'

They drag themselves out of the booth and stand over me. Hatch grabs the gun. He points the barrel at my head, hand on the trigger.

– *Snap*

My arms jolt.

'It ain't even loaded,' he says. 'Just couldn't leave it out there on the bike.'

Dennis squats down, looking me in the eye. He says, 'Kid, we know who you all are. You're Nate. And Jesse's girlfriend is... that slut with the name like someone's grandma, she's...' and he clicks his fingers.

'Iris,' says Hatch.

'That's right. Iris,' repeats Dennis. 'We know about Iris. We can keep her out of it... if we play our cards right. We don't need to visit her. She's a friend of yours, right?'

'Yes.'

'Good. Then there's the other guy isn't there? Foot? Shoe?'

'Sock,' I say.

'That's right, that's right,' says Dennis quietly. 'We been asking around. All the wind's blowing the same way. Everybody says you know Jesse better than anyone. So now you've got a couple of days to dig him up.'

'Or get our money,' says Hatch. 'Forty-five grand.'

'I don't even know what this is about.'

'Then you better find Jesse and ask him,' says Dennis.

He stands up and kicks me in the side, hard.

By the time I'm done wiping my eyes, they're gone.

Then there's just the boom of two motorbikes in the distance.

After a time, I check my watch.

9:42 p.m.

Still early. I get my things and walk up to the shower block because I have no idea what to do next. The hot water pelts down on me. An old man sings 'Sweet Caroline' to himself, two cubicles over and it creeps me out. He keeps circling back to the opening verse, never getting to the chorus, never finishing up. I think about jerking off but have to nix it. I can't concentrate through the singing.

I head back to the van.

I check my beeper. A dozen flashing messages.
10:11 p.m.
It's a Wednesday night in Gatton.
The dance is on tonight.

I walk through the back streets of campus until I hear 'Cotton Eye Joe' drifting through the darkness. I curse Jesse. I haven't been to the dance since first year. That we still have a dance – that we call it that – tells you everything you need to know about Gatton. This dance is held every Wednesday night, in a white, aluminum-clad shed. The shed sits a stone's throw from the campus club. The people who come to this thing drink six nights a week in the campus club, then one night in the shed, a couple of metres away. That's how it works. Agricultural students are the core regulars. But some of the more munted business students are there every week. And the girls – they all seem to be girls – studying horse-husbandry are into it as well. The horticulture burnouts only turn up when they're fundraising. Then there's the rest of us: anyone who needs a weed connection; anyone under eighteen; and anyone looking to get laid in a hurry. That's who's there.

I hate it.

Sonya Hamilton from my Sem One Microeconomics class is on the door tonight. She's wearing a white chambray shirt, collar popped. I didn't know this was her thing. She dressed different in class.

'Five dollars,' she says, as a greeting.

'I'm looking for someone, Sonya. Can I just pop in and then come back out?'

'Still costs five dollars. Do I know you?'

I helped Sonya out with some notes for that class.

'Yeah. It's Nate.'

'Ah yeah. Well, the Cattlemen's Club are raising money for the Bachelor and Spinster Ball so…'

'Then I'm definitely not paying.'

'It's still five dollars.'

There's no security so I walk through. As I do it, Sonya shouts something my way, but nothing else happens.

Inside, the dance is heaving. At least two hundred bogan dickheads are crammed into the courtyard adjoining the shed. They're all standing in packs, shouting at each other over the music. Half of them are wearing hats at night, including the women.

I head straight to the bathroom and join the line.

Craig Lewis spots me on his way out. He's loaded. Must be, because he stops and shakes my hand like we're old friends. His fingers are wet.

'Well, look at this,' he says. 'Someone must be *reaaaal* thirsty for some gash to come to this mess, and do you know who that person is?'

'It's not me. I'm here looking for Jesse.'

'Fucking Jesse…'

Craig sways a little. He looks like he's about to blurt out a bunch of stuff here in the crowded bathroom so I shut it down. 'I'll come find you.'

'Sure. Sure.'

I get to the front of the line and it's for the sink instead of the urinal. It's already half-clogged with piss and toilet paper. I use it anyway.

Outside, I run into Donna and Spencer. Donna's mashed. She hugs me and it lasts longer than it should. Spencer's no better. He looks like he can't stop the short two-step he's locked into.

'So, what are you two doing here?'

Donna says, 'We're on the last of that gear from Jesse. Spence here got the bright idea that coming to this Klan rally on pills might be good for a laugh.'

'Yeah,' says Spencer.

'How's that working out?'

'Some of them are kinda hot,' says Donna. 'It's weird.'

'Yeah,' says Spencer. He looks around.

'Tell Jesse we want more of this stuff,' says Donna.

'Is he here?'

'Bill Clinton saw him. That's what he said.'

That's actually the kid's name, the poor bastard.

'Willy?'

'Yeah,' says Spencer.

'So Jesse sold you this stuff?'

'What?' says Donna.

'The pills.'

'Sock hooked us up, but yeah. It's his shit.'

'Right.'

'You've got to try them,' says Donna.

Spencer says, 'Yeah.' He wipes his brow. The DJ plays 'Informer' by Snow and he starts moving his head in time to the intro. He dances a little faster.

'He likes this song,' says Donna.

'Licky boom-boom down,' says Spencer.

I go and find Willy Clinton. Willy dresses like a grunge cowboy: flannel, denim, elastic-sided boots. I like him but he isn't fond of me. He knows my ex, Chloe. They went to high school together. I thought our break-up was a lot harder on me than her but Willy's been short with me ever since.

'Hey, Willy, I'm looking for Jesse.'

'Jesse K?'

'That's right.'

'I saw him... uhmm... outside, or something.'

'Which way?'

He points.

'You sure?'

'Yeah, man. I like, know what the dude looks like. I've seen him before.'

I head out that way and find Craig instead. Craig's down the side of the shed talking to two girls. He's half in the dark, but it's him. As I come up, I notice four other guys standing in the shadows. The one closest to Craig is a guy I've had trouble with before. They call him Pinchy. The rest, I can't see all that well.

Craig lets out a long *Heeeeeey*.

'You got a moment?'

One of the girls with Craig gives me the up and down and screws her face up. She takes a bottle from one of the guys in the dark and has a long pull.

'You know these guys?' says Craig.

'Yeah,' I say.

'You don't know us,' says the girl with the bottle.

One of the guys laughs.

A cigarette ember flares. I recognise another face, some lunkhead from Riddell Hall. I sold to him on the winter break, when Craig was away. Jesse and I get along fine with Craig – he likes us, and he's a really weird guy – but he's also an ex-rodeo rider from Emerald, so he completely passes muster with the agricultural students. He pretty much only deals to the violent redneck hicks that Jesse and I avoid at all costs. Hicks like Pinchy.

Pinchy says, 'I know this retard.' He sounds fucked up. Last time we spoke like this, Pinchy dropped me with two punches. That's his idea of a negotiation.

Craig doesn't seem to notice any of this. 'You want a smoke, man?'

'Over there.' I walk to a chain-link fence across the street. Craig stays where he is and keeps on talking. Just when I think he's forgotten me, the others leave and he comes over.

'Nate, Nate, Nate, my mate.' He puts an arm around my shoulder. 'Everyone wants their weed and I don't have any.'

'Yeah. I'm in the same boat.'

'I've got another guy lined up. It's the new kid at the campus bookshop. He's from Lismore.'

Craig sparks up a joint. He's one of the few people I know who rolls his pot like Jesse. It's a promotional thing, like he can afford to waste it. He takes a long drag and passes it over.

I take a toke. It's good. It's our expensive stuff.

'Don't suppose you're holding some of this for me?'

'Just for you? Jesus. Times *are* tough,' says Craig.

He takes the joint back and drags on it.

'What were you doing at the bookshop, Craig?'

He chuckles. 'I got lost. And this Lismore kid can sell me a thirty-dollar ounce of grief, straight from the grower.'

'What about bud?'

'He's asking his dad. At the moment that's headed somewhere else. They're just trying to off-load the rest.'

'That doesn't help us much. I can barely move what's left of my grief.'

'Same. I got a plan though. I'm seeing a girl from food science. She reckons she can make space cake with all this leaf. We're going to tool around with it tomorrow.

But she's convinced it'll be good. She's had it before. You want in?'

'Sure. How much?'

'She wants half.'

We finish the joint and stand there together. The bass pulse coming from the shed starts to rattle me. The dark feels bad all of a sudden.

'Craig, there were some guys looking for Jesse the other night. They came to my caravan. They haven't talked to you, have they?'

'Nah man.' Craig burps. 'Why?'

'No reason.'

Craig doesn't need to know about Dennis and Hatch. He's a whole step further down the supply chain than I am. They'd have found him by now if they were going to.

'I gotta get another drink,' he says.

We walk back up to the entryway. There's a crowd outside now. The rugby guys have finished practice and they're standing around drinking XXXX Bitter tins, the empties piling up by a bin.

I take one last look at the scene and say to Craig, 'If Jesse shows, tell him to call me.'

Craig takes a second. He nods. Then I watch him squeeze himself into the crowd before I walk away.

I'm a few blocks from the dance when I hear a familiar voice.

'Hey, retard.'

Pinchy steps out of the dark. I hear giggling behind him. Women's voices.

He comes over.

'What do you want?'

'Nothing,' he says.

He's just standing there.

17

Then he says, 'You go to the dance?'

I nod.

'You don't normally go, right?'

'No.'

He moves fast. The blow lands in the fleshy part of my side and the air blasts out of me, warm in my throat.

I fall over.

Pinchy waits, then squats down beside me.

'Next time you go to the dance, which is hopefully never, you should fucking pay like everyone else. You owe Sonya five bucks, and an apology.'

He hocks up a mouthful of phlegm and spits it on me. It lands on my neck.

'And the Cattlemen send their regards.'

I can hear the girls laughing again.

His goodbye kiss is a dead leg.

I wait till I'm alone then stagger over to a street sign and hold onto it while I hurl.

Lights pass over me. A car approaches.

It slows. A shower of empties and insults:

Fucking faggot.

Soft, mate. You fucking soft cunt.

Go back to Brisbane.

I check the back window as they peel off.

The car's rammed full of people.

Six or seven guys.

One face staring back. I can't be sure it isn't Jesse. It looks just like him.

I'm slow and it's after midnight. I'm parked by Thynne Hall and when I get there, people are standing around in the gravel. 'Ten' by Pearl Jam blares out of a car stereo. A rocket arcs up into the air and explodes. Everyone cheers.

I just want to go home.

As I pass one of the groups, my name is called.

I ignore it but Samantha Kline appears. She slides in from the side and starts walking backwards in front of me.

'Thought that was you.'

She's a customer. Or was. I haven't seen her in a while.

'I'm all fucked up,' I say.

'Let me guess. You went to the dance?'

'Yeah.'

'Dude, you shoulda come here. The horties found a leftover keg from... some ball. Hey, stop, stop for a second, will ya?' She takes my face and brushes away my hair. 'Jesus, dude. You *are* kinda fucked up. You're bleeding... everywhere.'

'I think I scraped my head. I gotta get home.'

'Nah, you should come back, come to mine and I'll get you, like, cleaned up. You look like you killed someone. And there's a, what's it called... an RBT, that thing, on the other side of the ring road. So, you may as well come with me.'

I think about Dennis and Hatch. I think about my caravan.

The small piles of money.

A valley of hundreds.

A hill of tens.

A summit of fives.

I could sell everything I own and get nowhere.

Then I look at Sam and say, 'Okay.'

Sam is a hall warden in Thynne, believe it or not, so she has a little first-aid kit under her bed. Unfortunately, she's hammered so she's not much good with it. In the women's bathroom under the fluorescent lights, she makes her third attempt to plaster up my face. When that fails, a final year student waiting to use the shower takes over. The student fiddles with the bandage, then looks at it closer and recoils.

'What the... Sam, you dumb cunt. This is a pad.'

Sam looks at me in the mirror. 'Dude, sorry.'

The student finds a bandage. She has firm hands. It hurts like hell when she puts it on.

The night ends in Sam's bed. There are drinks first, a shared cigarette, some talk about school. She asks me about Chloe, and thinking about her makes everything hurt even worse so I lie and say something about it being time and the two of us drifting apart. *We want different things.* And I guess that's true enough. It's true for everyone. Everyone wants different things.

Even in this.

The light goes off as I undress her. Her breath is poison but she's warm. 'No, harder! Fuck,' she says at one point and pushes her face into the pillow.

A train snakes out in front of me like a bowed line in arid grasslands. Wind pushes on my face. The sun above is high and strong, blasting down on a world that looks like a playset.

It all pans past.

A hundred little houses and cars and roads and pubs and crossings.

People stand in their yards.

Kids sit on their bikes and wave.

I wave back because I'm sitting on a pile of coal, out in an open carriage, five hundred metres behind the only other human on this train.

I think I'm dreaming because my skin is covered in a film of matte black. I think it's soot, from the coal, but it feels thicker than that, like a wetsuit or Lycra. And my eyes are watering. Or I'm crying. Maybe I'm crying? I don't know. The only thing I know is that all this makes some sort of sense. I feel it in my gut, way deep down.

The dirt.

The black train.

The smiling, waving children.

The perfect miniature world.

There's a sense of order here, a linear sense of progression.

I deserve this. I know it somehow.

This is my Wednesday reduced down to crude signs and feelings.

I can't get off the train.

I can't stop it.

I'm here until something happens.

THURSDAY

I wake and run while Sam's still asleep. Outside her room, the dawn sun glistens in the lino at the end of Thynne Hall. It's almost beautiful and the whole campus feels subdued, in a coma.

My head pounds. My side and leg ache.

I have two matching bruises: two fist prints. I'm still moving slowly, almost limping.

Outside, I spot a garden hose in the brush and follow it back to the main. I hold the nozzle to my mouth and turn the tap. The nozzle stays dry but water sprays out of somewhere else, hitting my jeans. It takes a second to realise someone's slashed the hose. I take the broken opening and ram it into my mouth instead.

Thursday. September 9th. 1994.

'So now you've got a couple of days to dig him up.'

'Or get our money.'

I'm standing in the back room of the service station McDonald's out by the highway. I'm staring at my shift calendar on the wall.

What does a couple of days mean?

Till Sunday?

That's the deadline I draw up in my head.

Three days.

Maybe I can rob this place? Would it work?

I look closer at today's date: I'm rostered on tonight.

The day manager comes by. She stands beside me and says, 'Don't suppose you're holding?' Her name's Rachel. She's a big woman. Married. Has a bunch of kids. She's holding onto the tail end of a PhD thesis, but not the scholarship.

'I'm dry,' I say.

'Damn.'

She gives me a light pat on the shoulder then orders one of the new guys to make me breakfast. The poor kid reminds her that breakfast service has finished. It's 10:42 a.m.

'What did I say about taking orders?' says Rachel.

The kid sighs. 'You said –'

'That's right! Now, you either make him breakfast or you fuck me out back, against the ice locker. Clear?'

The kid shuffles off to his work station.

'Jesus, Rachel.'

'Oh, give me a break. I've been here all night.'

I sit in the McDonald's driveway and wait for a pause in the traffic. A horn blares behind me. Crossing the Warrego Highway in my car is no small thing. I drive a 1988 Daihatsu Charade. The auto. It accelerates like a ride-on lawnmower, zero to a hundred in two to three minutes.

The traffic flies past.

A truck.

Two white sedans.

A ute with a quad bike in the tray.

Then the break comes.

More horns. I put my foot flat to the floor.

The highway takes me east around the crop fields abutting campus, then past the long flats to the Gatton

Bypass and into town. The caravan park I live in is on the edge of town and when I get there, I pull into the same space I took the car out of yesterday. These spots aren't reserved, it's just that no one really comes here. I get out and cut up around the site office to avoid Graham and I'm walking along the far side of the park, keeping an eye out, when Becky Powell knocks on the window of her van. Becky's a student too. She waves me over.

'Hey, the cops were looking for you,' she says.

'What? Why?'

'Don't know. They stopped me on my way back from the laundry. Asked if I'd seen you.'

'What did you say?'

'That I hadn't seen you.'

'Thanks.'

Sure enough, there's a business card jammed into the rim of my caravan door. A white cardboard rectangle with a police shield in the corner. There's a name there, some constable. On the back, in biro, there's a note:

Give me a call when you get the chance.

I put the card in my wallet.

I call around and get nowhere. No one's seen Jesse. I make a list on a piece of paper: names, addresses. Leads, I guess. It's all going down onto the back of that flyer from the previous day.

I've been carrying it around.

Missing: Maya Kibby

I stare at the awkward photo of her again.

I knew her.

Jesse's house sits in the backstreets behind the showgrounds adjoining Gatton's shabby golf course. He's one of the only people I know who lives on his own. His father hooked it up. A family friend, a private lease, the whole deal. I've spent a lot of time here in this house. We all have.

For a drug dealer, Jesse doesn't give a fuck about security. He sleeps with the doors open and stores his money in a plastic ice-cream container by the bed. He's loose like that. But today, the house is locked up tight, meaning he's probably still out of town. I get down on my hands and knees and peer under his garage door, looking for his car. It's in there. I look in through the windows too. Then I knock again, for no real reason.

Nothing.

Silence.

He's not home.

There's a share house not far from Jesse's we call the Hospital. It's the place to go if you need something on prescription but they're not med students.

A kid they call Doctor Bowen answers the door. 'Whoa, Nate. How's it...' He trails off, nodding.

'What are you guys doing?'

'Oh, you know,' says the Doctor. He squints out at the street. 'Still going from last night.'

He drifts back into the house.

I follow.

The Hospital has a long living room along one side and a kitchen up one end. They've got it dark today: old blankets and sheets plastered over the windows. Five of them are sitting around a coffee table, all men. I recognise some of them but they barely notice me coming in.

The Doctor eases himself into a busted white leather couch. 'Scoot over man, shit.'

They have an old record player wired in. A guitar solos over an organ. It sounds like *The War of the Worlds* or some shit.

'What is this?' I say.

One of them looks at me, then at the speakers, then at the Doctor.

The Doctor thinks about it. 'We can't tell you,' he says.

'Okay. Any of you guys heard from Jesse? I thought he might be round here?'

'Jesse?' says the Doctor. 'Oh right, yeah. That guy. Maybe.'

'We should show him,' says another guy.

Another one starts nodding. 'Yeah. We should. It's the right thing to do. He can handle it.'

The Doctor sighs. 'Do you want to see something, Nate? I guess you do. Come over here. Come,' he says.

The Doctor pours a shot of Wild Turkey into a coffee mug, then mutters to himself. 'What next, what next...' He reaches down beside the couch and pulls up an old soda canister. 'Fuck, fuck, fuck, where are the –'

'Here,' says one of the guys and slings a whipped cream bulb across the room.

The Doctor somehow catches it and screws the bulb into the canister. He presses down a lever and the canister hisses. When it's done, he puts it down beside the coffee mug of bourbon and leans forward, retrieving a bag of pot from under a magazine. He pinches off a bud and carefully dusts it off. 'There's something in with this hundy and I don't know what it is,' he says.

I pick up the bag and take a look. It looks like our good stuff. The gear we had a fortnight back.

The Doctor packs a small pipe and says:

'There are four Bs.'

He points:

The bourbon.

The bulb.

The bud.

It's only three by my count but I don't say anything.

'We've all done them,' says one of the other guys. He hunches forward and rests his head on a shaky hand. He looks a little tense, like he's excited.

'You did want to know something, right?' says the Doctor.

'Know what?' I say.

'There's no explaining it,' says the nervous one.

'There's no explaining it,' repeats the Doctor.

'And I need to, ahhh...' and I point at the line-up of things on the coffee table.

'One after the other, as fast as possible. Doctor's orders. It's helped everyone here, hasn't it? Hasn't it? We've all found something we were looking for.'

They all murmur, *Yes, yes.*

'It's a bit early for this sort of thing,' I say.

The Doctor yawns. 'Then we can't help you.'

'What's the fourth B?'

He looks confused, then narrows his eyes. 'Ooooh, that. It's got to be seen. Can't be shown.'

'Has anyone seen Jesse? Is he here?'

The Doctor frowns. He waves a hand at the coffee table and says, 'As your Doctor, I'm prescribing *these* things, then we'll talk. You know... you shouldn't, like, ignore my advice.'

There's something going on.

I sit down, cross-legged, at the coffee table. 'Any specific order?'

'There's no order to anything,' says some guy who's been quiet up till now.

So I do the shot first.

It burns, all the way in. I hate shots.

Bulbs aren't my thing either but I'm not new to it. While the bourbon is still hurting me, I put my mouth over the canister nozzle and push on the trigger, inhaling nice and slow.

Tunnel vision.

The world tilts forward.

Echoes.

I used to be the happiest person I knew.

I remember Iris being that way too.

We must have spent half our lives as kids just walking

31

around at dusk. We ran down one street after the other back then, all those cheap houses on the edge of the Eagleby scrub.

It was warm.

My vision opens back out.

Someone hands me the pipe.

A lighter appears.

I just breathe.

It sure doesn't taste like our stuff. They're right. There's something else in there, something chemical.

I keep on breathing.

Then I hold.

My face feels slightly numb. I imagine the skin there being cold to touch. The colour of the room is all fucked up now. *They need to open a window.* In a beam of light seeping in, I can see dust floating, millions of tiny pieces of tiny dust. *This is their skin, right? They need to clean this fucking –*

They need to open a –

I exhale and the smoke makes me think I'm rolling back rather than breathing out.

It's definitely not our stuff. Backed with something else.

Everyone's smiling at me.

The Doctor looks satisfied.

I say, 'Now what?'

'Who wants to take him?' says the Doctor.

'Hallway?' says one of the others.

The Doctor nods. He's already packing another cone.

The nervous guy from before appears beside me. 'You... you all good, man?'

'Yeah, I think so.'

'Come with me.'

The guy leads me up the living room and through the

kitchen into a long hallway of doors. There, he points down to the far end of the hallway where a colourful square poster is stuck to the wall. 'Go and look at it,' he says.

I walk towards the poster.

The guy stays in the kitchen behind me, almost like he's scared to come further. About halfway along the hall, I feel weird and stop. I turn around and look back.

'Keep going, man. Go to the thing, and look at it.'

I approach and stand there.

It's not a poster. It's an album cover. *Oneness: Silver Dreams & Golden Reality.* A yellow relief, a line of infinite sitting Buddhas disappearing into a horizon point.

The fourth B is Buddha.

Bourbon.

Bulbs.

Bud.

Buddha.

I look closer:

Devadip Carlos Santana.

'You asked what we were listening to,' calls the guy from the kitchen.

I turn around.

'Fucking Santana?'

'Yeah man. Just look into it, man. Go, go into it. It's forever. It goes and goes and goes. There's no place where it stops, not ever. Like, very... infinite.'

I turn back and stare into the album cover.

'What do you see?' he calls.

'Nothing.'

'Just keep going then. I'm gonna leave you to it.'

He steps out of the doorway.

I take his advice. I stare harder at it. The image doesn't morph or change. Whatever the weed's cut with, it's not a hallucinogen. I keep on staring. As I let my eye travel along the line of Buddhas, I start to feel as if I'm travelling down into myself, almost like there really is a connection.

Then I come back to reality.

These guys are fucking kooks.

I pull the record cover off the wall. Underneath it, taped to the wallpaper is a black-and-white image. It's a grainy photograph on a piece of A4 paper, a video still from a computer screen, run off on a dot-matrix printer. It takes a moment to make out: a woman, her eyes squeezed shut, a cock in her mouth. Her face is obscured by long dark hair but something about her feels familiar. A line of text sits along the top of the page. Backslashes, half-words, numbers. Nonsense. I don't know what it is.

I tear the thing down and put it in my pocket.

Then I give the hallway bedrooms a sweep.

There's a naked couple sleeping in one.

A bucket bong by an empty bed in another.

In a closet, there's a pile of trash shaped into a pyramid.

The bathroom's barren. Just empty ice bags.

There's a master suite filled with prescription bottles and spent tissues.

But nothing else. And no Jesse.

No signs of him. Nothing he owns. No sense of him having camped out here.

I find a side door and step out. I stand there a moment on the Hospital's rear deck and listen. I can hear the Doctor holding court in the other room. His voice is loud and authoritative. It takes a while but I catch the gist of it. He's lecturing them about the end of *Apocalypse Now*.

The dashboard clock reads 11:38 a.m., and I shouldn't be driving. The sun is high. Heat wafts off the windscreen. I'm driving pretty fast.

I've got a lit cigarette draped out the side of my mouth and I don't even remember lighting it. I don't even smoke tobacco.

That fucking gear from the Hospital.

I ease off.

Johnny Mouth aka Johnny M. aka Silent John aka John-John is next on my list. He's a different person to everyone who knows him and I don't like any of them. All the Johns and Johnnys, they all talk too much.

'Oh, oh, oh it's Business Nate, knocking on my door, interrupting my *21 Jump Street*. You wanna come in? Come in, watch the show with me. It's barely started. It's the one where Hanson and Hoffs go undercover in the black school and Penhall does stand-up. You seen it? It's like Gatton, man. Like, how things are for me and stuff –'

John's half-Vietnamese and half-hick. He told me about it once.

'– And then, oh man, come in, you're missing it. Look at that girl! Damn man, damn –'

I stay at the door.

He's got a tall marijuana plant sitting right there in the

living room. John's got to be the dumbest dealer Jesse has on the books, but somehow he gets it done. And he's the Ipswich connect. Good for a couple of ounces out that way every shipment. For some reason, people respond to him down there. I don't know why. They're the most racist people I've ever met.

'Oh shit, look man, look at –'

'You seen –'

'Jesse? Yeah, man. Out at Sock's place, night before last.'

'His house or the drive-in?'

'Drive-in.'

'Night before last?'

'Or the night before the night before last, man. I don't know, man. I get so confused. *So confused!* I'm really bad with dates, times, fucking numbers, I don't even know what year it is, I don't –'

He's doing my head in. None of the lines in his house look straight to me. The place is sliding. I touch my forehead. It's wet with sweat.

I hear myself say, 'You holding?'

'Out, man. Clean out of everything except that plant right there. Look at that thing. I mean really, I mean come on –'

He's still talking to me as I take the path back to the car.

'– I mean, oh hey, Nate, hey, where you going, man? You're missing some good –'

I don't look back.

I get in the car and close the door.

Sock works for Jesse just like I do. Between him, Craig and I, we've got Gatton stitched up. Sock does the locals. Craig does the jocks and cowboys. I do everyone in between.

There's not much else to say about Sock. He's a chubby weirdo with a penchant for Hawaiian shirts and reef sandals. He has a strange jealous vibe to him, kind of secretive and odd, especially with Iris. He doesn't stand a chance with Iris, and he has a girlfriend (by some miracle), but he never misses an opportunity to be around her. It gets tiring. He's got these beady little rat eyes that he squints at me every time I walk in the room, as if to say, *Oh, you're here, again.*

Sock's girlfriend is Mandy Lowenfield. She lives in an old drive-in theatre on the outskirts of Gatton. People think this place is a myth but it's not. The drive-in's been a student share house for a decade. Mandy and her roommate Gemma (the polar opposite of Mandy: hot, from Byron Bay) have both lived out there for a while. They don't talk it up. It's not a novelty to them. The house is a nightmare, actually: a stuffy brick box with a flat roof, sitting in the centre of a bitumen car park. It's the drive-in's old candy store and projection house, a real shithole.

I park out on the street and get into the drive-in through a hole in the fence. As I come down to the house, my vision swims. In the distance, white-hot glare radiates off the old movie screen, something that now resembles a half-collapsed billboard. I feel desperately thirsty and tired from the Doctor's fucked-up weed but I keep moving.

As I come round the back of the house, I find Mandy and Gemma standing out on the lot, shooting at an old steel drum with an air rifle.

As I get closer, Mandy points the rifle at me and says, 'What do you want?'

'I'm looking for Sock.'

'It's not like he lives here, you know?'

'Do you know where he is?'

Mandy withdraws the rifle. She re-pumps it and points it back at the drum.

I look at Gemma. 'Do you know where he is?'

She shrugs. She doesn't like Sock. Or me.

'Heard Chloe dumped you,' says Mandy.

She pulls the trigger on the rifle.

Crack.

A spark fires off the drum.

'That's right.'

'She was too good for you anyhow, Nate. She's like, some super-nerd and shit, gonna work in a lab or something.'

'I'm halfway through a business degree.'

'Yeah, in selling drugs and being a fuckwit.'

They both laugh at that.

'Mandy, do you know when Sock's going to be back? Or is he just... gone?'

'He's in Toowoomba.'

'Is Jesse with him? Have either of you seen Jesse?'

Gemma says, 'I've seen Jesse. He was at Coles the other day, buying some stuff.'

'When was that?'

'I don't know. Last week.'

'Okay. Can I use your toilet?'

Mandy swings the rifle back in my direction. 'Are you going to touch any of our stuff?'

She pulls the trigger.

The pellet goes wide.

'Shit, Mandy!'

'Of course you can use *the toilet*. Why are you such a little pussy all the time, Nate. Just fucking use the toilet.'

I go in. The house is a wreck. Mandy and Gemma have never been big on cleaning but today they look a month overdue on having done anything at all: the dishes, the garbage, the laundry, the kitty litter. Every room is a new set of trash piles.

I don't even bother with the bathroom. I take a mouthful of water from the kitchen tap and start casing the bedrooms. No notes or bus tickets or receipts or familiar pieces of clothing or air mattresses or any sign that Jesse has been camped out. There's a pile of video equipment in one of the cupboards, old cameras stenciled with *Laidley State High School*, a tripod and such, but not much else. Mandy and Gemma are enrolled in degrees but I can't see any sign of them studying. No books or desk or computer. They're idiots. And as if to prove it, they've got that Maya Kibby *Missing Person* flyer stuck to their fridge. They've drawn sunglasses on her and added a speech bubble over her mouth.

Maya's saying: *I'm Dead! Boo! Hoo!*

I take out my list and turn it over.

I compare the two flyers, side by side.

They're the same.

*T*hey knew Maya Kibby was dead when a dog found her. Kenny from Intro to Property Law – he knew the family who owned the dog. Apparently it was gone half the night. The owner's family was worried. They're out there, in their pyjamas with flashlights, looking for the dog. A few hours later, the youngest son sees it coming in from the dark, dragging something. The kid yells the dog's name.

'And it's got this bloody stump in its mouth,' says Kenny. 'It was her arm, dude. Can you imagine? And you want to know what's worse?'

I don't but Kenny doesn't care.

'They had to shoot the dog. Apparently you can't have a farm dog around once they've tasted human flesh. It fucks them up. Once they've had it, that's it, game over.' And then Kenny keeps talking about it, going through the whole story a second time, telling me how terrible it is that the dog had to die.

I make deliveries, off-loading the last of my garbage weed. Everyone wants to talk. Everyone wants something other than what they're getting. I'm sick of explaining it but I explain it anyway. *We're all waiting on a package.* But we're not because Jesse is everyone's connection and now no one knows where Jesse is.

As I'm driving into the early afternoon sun, I start to straighten out a little. I realise that this might be it: my last week as a low-grade drug dealer. I concentrate on that – on the end of my business – because hiding behind it is that other situation with the bikers.

Getting desperate, I go back to Jesse's house and knock on the door. I peer in through the windows and call the landline from a phone booth around the corner. Then I walk back and try again for no reason because he's not home.

Back in my caravan, with *Superunknown* in the cassette player and my shirt off, I have a cone or two and drink the leftover cask wine. I'm not sure what else to do. Every hour, on the hour, I go up to the phone in the rec room and check my beeper and make calls. I start hitting Sock's beeper more often than Jesse's. I stop returning messages from my customers. It's getting to be all or nothing, and a few sticks of grief here and there won't change it.

I start thinking about the nothing options:
Run.
Leave Gatton.
Sell everything I own.
Rob the McDonald's.
Use the business card. Go to the cops.
I walk back through the caravan park in the dusk humidity and I revise my list:
~~Run.~~
~~Leave Gatton.~~
~~Sell everything I own.~~
~~Rob the McDonald's.~~
~~Use the business card. Go to the cops.~~
The fucking cops, no way.
The list is a fantasy. None of it adds up to anything good.
Like a crazy person pacing and muttering to myself, I head back to the rec room and back to the phone and I call Iris.
'You've got to come round. Things are all fucked up.'
'I know,' she says.
For five seconds that's enough.
I wait.

Another sip of wine from a plastic cup. Another cone, the cherry bright in the blur. *Siamese Dream* on the stereo. It's dark out. I can't remember the last time I ate. I can't remember the last time I spoke to my parents. I have no memory, at all, of my last relaxed moment.
I look at my kitchen bench and think about Dennis and Hatch and the rifle.
The police business card is in my hand:
Constable Alexander Sennett, it says.
Give me a call when you get the chance.
'Fuck off,' I say out loud, to myself.

There's some history here. It goes way back. I hate cops and I figure, *Give me a call when you get the chance* pretty much equals, *We want to bust you for possession and distribution with intent, please call the station at your convenience.*

'No way.'

I might not be thinking this through properly.

It's too much.

I can't remember where I woke up this morning.

I have assignments due.

I need money and I can't get it.

Thursday has been a waste of time and time is the last thing, on a long list of things, I don't have.

Iris comes at 11:03 p.m. This is how she is. She's never been one to rush to anything. She steps up into my caravan without knocking, then takes a look around, sees me half-passed-out in the breakfast nook, and keeps looking like I'm part of the fabric.

'I'm dying for a piss,' she says.

The van is small and I hear her cough and spit into the bathroom. When she reappears she says, 'I see things have been progressing over here,' and then goes to the closet in the van's little hallway and pulls out a folding camp chair. When she comes to the van, she always sits on this particular chair, having lifted it from a garage sale a few months ago. Iris is not a tidy person but she finds the caravan park especially depressing – *dirty, wretched, povo* – and this chair of hers is part of that. It's her space. It's cordoned off. She sits there, same as ever: light brown hair pulled back, impossibly pale skin. Beautiful, I guess. And the *only* reason she sits there, in *her* chair, in a place like mine, is because we grew up together.

'Any word?' I say.

She lights a cigarette, exhales. She's shaky, too, I note. 'Nope.'

'No Jesse?'

'Fuck Jesse.'

'Okay. I, ah…'

'You sound munted.'

'So do you. You okay?'

'I'm fine.' She grinds the cigarette out even though she's barely started on it. 'How's your business?'

'I'm fucked. I wasn't… holding back any… supply.'

'Aren't you studying business?'

'Yeah, I… ah. You really don't have any, do you? Even my… even my own stash is almost done.'

'Nate, I said on the phone. I'm out. This is going to fuck you up with your dad, isn't it? The house thing.'

'I can't even talk to Dad, at the moment.'

'Maybe I can help?'

'You?'

'I've got some money saved up.'

'Ri, no.' I go to the sink and run the water. Wet my face again. 'How much do you have?'

'A couple of grand. Is it that bad?'

'Don't worry about it.'

'How's Maccas?' she says. 'Haven't seen you out there in a while.'

Iris keeps the sort of hours where she ends up buying her basics from the BP servo attached to the McDonald's.

'Christ!'

'What?' she says.

'I'm rostered on.'

'When? Tonight?'

I check my watch.

'Fifteen minutes ago.'

Iris shakes her head. 'Get your things. I'll drive you.'

***

The inside of Iris's car is completely black and there aren't a lot of streetlights in Gatton. As we drive, she glances away from the road and reaches up under the steering wheel into the plastic casing there. She grabs something and rattles it. The dash lights spring back to life.

'That's better,' she says.

This is the car we came to Gatton in. She refuses to junk it.

'So, why *were* you looking for Jesse?' I say.

'What?'

She's bluffing.

I say, 'You called me. You were looking for him.'

'When?'

'On the phone.'

'Yesterday?'

'I think so. I think it was yesterday. Look, Ri, if you and Jesse split up because of what happened the other –'

'No.'

'No, what?'

'No, we've talked about that already.'

'We have *not* talked about it.'

Iris laughs. It's a harsh, exasperated sound. 'Christ, Nate. Just…'

'What?'

'Just fucking –'

'Okay, okay. You do whatever you like.'

'Okay, thanks, Nate. I think I might do that anyhow.'

She steers the car off the road, along the gravel shoulder of the highway and into the servo. She parks by the McDonald's doorway but I don't get out straight away. Instead, I sit there and say, 'You haven't seen anyone hanging around, have you? Like, some guys?'

'What guys?'

'No one in particular.'

'Have *you*?' says Iris.

I look out the window at the restaurant fluoros and say no. I wait a beat and add, 'Things are weird right now, aren't they?'

'Things are always weird with us,' she says, too quickly. 'What guys, Nate?'

'No one. It's nothing. I don't know what I'm going to do if Jesse doesn't magically reappear.'

'You'll work it out.'

She doesn't actually believe this. She's looking out the windscreen now, waiting for me to leave.

I reach for the latch. 'Thanks for the ride.'

She nods, still looking away.

I get out.

'Hey?'

I stop. 'Yeah?'

'Whatever's going on... just try and stay out of it, Nate. Please. Don't let yourself get mixed up in Jesse's bullshit. Just don't.'

'You know, sometimes you're like a broken record.'

Iris backs the car up.

I wave as she drives off but she doesn't wave back.

The girl on fries takes one look at me – at my half-limping walk and my completely stoned and drunk face – and says, 'Fucking hell. Your eyes are practically bleeding. I think they *are* bleeding.'

'Sorry... sorry I'm late.'

'Oh, man,' she says.

She calls the night manager over and he laughs as soon as he sees me. They both stand there, checking me out.

'What do you reckon?' says the girl.

'Crown duty,' says the manager.

'No. Come on,' I plead.

'Dude,' says the manager. 'You know the drill.'

I know it.

They go and get the box of cardboard birthday crowns we use for children's parties and take me to the cold room with it.

The fries girl opens the door. 'Good luck,' she says.

I walk in.

'See you in a bit.'

The cold room is a white refrigerator lined with the things no one ever wants to see: pus-coloured pancake mix, a colostomy bag full of chocolate sundae topping, open boxes of identically shaped frosted-white meat patties. We also keep the Christmas decorations in there, though I'm not sure why.

At first, the chill isn't so bad. I drag over a black milk crate and sit on it. I make one of the crowns and put it on my head. Then I sit there, king of the world, hunched over with my head against my closed fists, trying to sober up.

It's 11:57 p.m.

*M*y mother sits at the kitchen table in the dank house I grew up in and shakes her head. She's frustrated, angry. She gets it. She understands why I'm leaving and wants me to go, but she can't put it aside. She stares at her Garfield coffee mug – an old birthday present – and waits, which is what we're all doing.

Dad potters around. He fusses with things in the kitchen, drying each part of a saucepan set.

I sit there.

'You'll call when you're settled, won't you?' my mother says.

'I'll call.'

'I don't know what I'm going to do. I don't know what I'm going to do tonight even,' she says.

Dad says, 'We'll work something out, luv. Maybe we can rent a video. There's plenty to do.'

My mother shrugs it off. She stares back at the mug.

All my stuff for university is piled up in the garage: an army surplus duffle full of clothes, a box of books, a box of stationary, a box of linen.

I hear Iris and her car come up the drive.

I go to the window and check. 'It's Ri.'

My mother doesn't move.

Dad and I go out to the garage. I open the tilter door and there's Iris. She looks pretty bad as well. She unlocks *the boot of her car and my father puts one of the boxes in. When he's done, he gives her a hug.*

'You kids are going to be fine,' he says, still holding her. 'Your mum okay?'

'She's at work,' says Iris.

'I'll give her a call tonight,' says Dad.

'I can't stop you.'

We put the rest of my stuff in the car. Then I go back to the kitchen on my own.

'All packed,' I say.

Mum nods.

'Mum?'

She gets up but knocks the table. The Garfield mug rolls in slow motion down onto the tiles and smashes open.

We both squat down to pick up the pieces.

She's crying and I'm holding her but she doesn't stop sweeping the mug together. Coffee is leaching into the trim of her nightgown. One of her fingers is cut open.

'Mum?'

She keeps going. I can't stop her. I stand up and watch her scratch at the floor.

'I've got to go.'

She keeps going, picking through every tiny shard, soaking up every drip of liquid with her nightgown, crying like she's choking it out of herself and like she wants it to keep coming.

She's been like this since my brother died.

Iris has loose change stolen from her mother's purse so we take the tollway up through the back end of Kingston. The road winds through parks and hills and down chutes of bronze noise-abatement walls. It puts us out at Wacol, after the prison there, then winds onto the Warrego Highway and into the long stretch of farming land to Gatton.

The day is bright.

We look at it, or pretend to.

Neither of us say much.

By Hattonvale, I feel like we should try and brush off the bad vibe. As we pass the Schultes Meat Tavern, I remember this thing and start saying it. 'My grandfather and grandmother drove me past a butcher like that once, on the way out to Beaudesert, where Mum's people are from.'

'Right,' says Iris.

'And my grandfather said this thing, it was so weird. He did this bit. He says, I went into that butcher once. I wanted to buy some sausages. And when I was in there, I bent down to look at the sausages and I noticed the butcher had a piece of string hanging from his fly. You know, off his pants there, so I asked him what it was for.'

'Oh god,' says Iris.

'I know, I know. And so the butcher, he doesn't answer straight away. He just points to this little sign on the wall that says All Meat in This Store Is Handled With Tongs. *So my grandfather says, I don't get it. And the butcher says, Well, when I go to the toilet, I use the piece of string to lower my fly and my dick flops out and then I can piss. And my grandfather, he's like, That sounds reasonable. But Nate, he says, I don't know why but I just kept looking at the meat and something was bugging me. Then it dawned on me and I said to him, If you use the string to open your fly, how do you put your dick back in your pants. And the butcher, he points back to the sign and says, With the tongs.'*

It's not a great joke but it works.

We're nervous, so we're both still crying when Iris comes over the hill into Gatton Shire. In the distance, we see it: the sparse university campus we'll call home for the next three years.

FRIDAY

After three hours sleep, I sit in the back corner of my ten o'clock Macroeconomics B class. My Indian tutor – a black business shirt tucked into black slacks all covered in white chalk dust – works on a four-quadrant graph that absolutely none of us understand. A guy up front is holding his head. The girl next to me is crossing out every word in the textbook, one word at a time.

The clock ticks.

'... Now, remember, our demand for pizza is plotted here, as it always is, and thus...'

My tutor is pointing to the first quadrant and a line marked *Quality of Pizzas Purchased*.

Price and supply.

I understand that part.

I take the *Missing: Maya Kibby* flyer from my pocket, look at her then turn it over and check my list:

~~*The Hospital.*~~

~~*J.M.*~~

~~*Sock.*~~

Campus.

Food hall.

Keg party.

I haven't looked on campus. Jesse has an afternoon class and a deal to make there. He might show up. And it's a Friday; the food science students have a house party on Fridays. That's also an option.

It's not a long list.

If he doesn't show today, I'm fucked. Jesse isn't one to spend his weekends in Gatton. He goes to the city. And I don't want to tell any of this to the bikers. Just thinking about it makes me twitch.

'... So the elasticity goes up as people switch to substitute pizzas...'

The guy in front of me is picking at splinters in his desk now, completely lost.

I'm hungover. I feel like I'm looking through the blackboard.

The tutor's voice is receding down a deep reverberant hole.

My fucking head.

I check my pager. I call my best customers from the phone box outside F Block and only a few of them pick up.

I apologise.

I reorganise.

They're still bugging out.

One girl drank her bong water.

Some other guy tells me his pipe looks brand-new. That's how many times he's scraped it.

If Jesse has called anyone, it'll be Craig, to check the weekend orders. So I call Craig and his roommate tells me he's out in the yard.

I wait. I stay on the line.

The roommate comes back inside and says, 'He wants to take it out there. I gotta plug in the extension lead. Call us back in five.' The roommate sounds flustered, like this is important. I have no idea why they're doing any of this, but Craig is a bit like that. He has projects, big ideas.

I go into the F Block reception and take a long drink from the water cooler. There's a ragtag collage of posters on the noticeboard above the bubbler:

Student Life's car wash.

A fridge and washer for sale.

Textbooks for trade.

I go back out and call Craig back.

'Nate, you'll never guess where I am!'

'In the back yard of your house, on the phone?'

'Dude, how did you do that?'

'I'm in the future, Craig.'

'What?' He sounds serious. He's out of it.

'Craig, what are you doing out there in the yard?'

'Don't you know?'

'No.'

'I'm sitting on a green plastic chair and I feel... great. I think Carrie has unlocked something pretty special here, man. Hey Carrie... hey, no, no, no, don't do that, oh shit... Oh shit, okay.'

'You there?'

'We've got a fire going, man.'

It's thirty degrees in the shade during bushfire season.

'Carrie just pulled one of the neighbour's fence palings off for kindling,' says Craig.

'Okay. Is this the space-cake thing?'

'I think it's the space-cake thing.'

'You selling it yet?'

'I don't know if I can bring money into this, Nate. It's too important. I've been high for...' I can hear him conferring with Carrie. She sounds even worse, like she's drooling. 'Ages. Maybe. A long time.'

'Craig, I need something. I need Jesse.'

Craig talks to Carrie again. 'She has more. Come over. If you need help, Nate, we can help you but you have to come over... No babe, you're right, we *want* to help you, Nate. Come round. And ah, can you bring something, like donuts or...'

More muffled banter.

'Carrie wants a tray of Neenish tarts, from the Coles and... what? A banana. Some bananas. I don't know, man, I don't know. I don't know any –'

I hang up.

I walk down to my old dormitory hall and it's the same. There's a girl in the upstairs of the C Wing they call Red Light (ginger, gets around) and Red Light buys Craig's gear in bulk. I try her room first. She isn't in, but on the door of her room she has a little miniature whiteboard and a marker, for messages.

Her mother called.

Sully came by, he wants to come back later.

And then there's Jesse's handwriting:

We're off for tonight. Call me.

Or at least I think it's Jesse's writing. It looks like it.

I go across the hall and knock on the opposing door.

A girl answers. I don't know her. 'What? I'm studying.'

'Have you seen...' I can't remember Red Light's real name, so I point. 'Her, today?'

'Rosie?'

I nod.

The girl steps out into the hallway. She's wearing silk pyjama bottoms and slippers. 'If you can't hear her getting butt-fucked by a footballer, she's probably not in there. That's all she does up here.' The girl says this loud, into Red Light's door.

'Okay. You seen a guy called Jesse around?'

'I don't know who that is.' She looks at me, into my eyes. 'Doesn't anyone study anymore?'

I try the other halls of residence, drifting from wing to wing, checking in with people I either know or I know Jesse knows. It's awkward. There's a lot of *Nah, man* and the door closing. Lots of people packing for the weekend. By midday, the only students left on campus are the ones who live here full-time. That used to be me. I don't really go home for the weekends either.

In Pitt Hall, I get desperate and try a girl I know Jesse used to sleep with. She was the one before Iris. Her name's Jessica Dyer. Jess and Jesse. That was never going to work. When she opens her door, she doesn't look happy to see me.

'You remember me?'

'Yeah.'

'I've lost Jesse. Was wondering if you'd seen him?'

'Why would I have seen him? I haven't seen anyone, especially him.'

She starts crying. She's standing there, tears streaming out.

'You okay?'

'What?'

She slams the door closed.

I'm walking back down the hall when I see a guy watching me. It's all girls upstairs at Pitt but he's standing in the doorway of a room in his underwear, scratching himself like he's just woken up.

'How is she?' he says.

'Who?'

He looks up the hallway. 'Jess. She's been like that for ages.'

'Why?'

'Her friend got killed.'

'Maya Kibby?'

'Yeah, man.'

That doesn't make a lot of sense. Maya was a local girl. She wasn't a student.

'How'd she know her?'

'Dunno,' says the guy.

'And she's still... like that?'

'Yeah.'

It feels weird.

I knew Maya. She worked the register in the highway servo attached to the McDonald's. She stood across from me for endless nights of shift work. We didn't talk much and we weren't friends, and I didn't really like her – she was kind of a bitch – but I knew her, I guess. I'd overheard her gossip. How she thought the day guys were lifting from the till, how she hated various ex-school friends, how lame she thought the students were, how she loved certain movies and how she was saving up to get the fuck out of Gatton. I remember the first night at work without her too, and the quiet, weird nights when she was still missing. I knew all this about her and had spent all this time with her but I didn't feel anything specific about her death. I wasn't upset like Jess Dyer in Pitt Hall. I didn't miss Maya at all.

I eat lunch in the refec with the boarders. I lived on campus my first year in Gatton and the food is worse than I remember. Today, it's some sort of grey chicken pie with soft vegetables and warm orange juice on the side. I'm on my own until Sam from the other night slides her tray onto the table beside me.

'Look at this,' she says.

'Hey.'

'No call, no kiss goodbye, no nothing.' She's smiling, laughing almost. 'How's the face?'

'Sore.'

'What are you doing on campus?'

'I come to class.'

'That's right. You're the diligent one.'

Sam cleans her knife and fork with a napkin. 'I had fun the other night.'

'Me too,' I say, although I'm not sure I did. She looks good. She has a pair of denim overall shorts on, a purple singlet underneath. Her breasts are tucked in there, stretching the fabric. I don't remember much of her from the other night. I can't picture her naked. But I want to now.

'You hanging around for the weekend?' she says.

I nod. 'I'm kinda fucked until I find Jesse.'

'Right. I forgot, I slept with a drug dealer.'

'It's not like I'm...' I'm about to say *a drug dealer* but I stop.

'You dabble,' she says.

'I need the money.'

'Doesn't everyone.'

'Why don't I sell to you anymore?'

'Gave it up,' she says. 'I'm not sure a drug that I can smoke every day and no one bats an eyelid is the drug for me.'

'Fair enough.'

Sam takes a mouthful of salad. We eat together for a while. A guy stops by the table and asks if I'm holding. I tell him: tomorrow. The guy walks off.

'Don't you already have a job?' says Sam, out of nowhere. 'I mean, you work at Maccas, right?'

'Yeah.'

'So you need two jobs?'

'Yeah.'

'Are you working on a Fabergé egg collection I don't know about? You're not paying your fees up-front, are you?'

'Family stuff. My mum's sick.'

'That's nice.' Sam chews it over. She looks around the room. 'What is it?'

'A long story.'

Sam touches the hair behind her ear. She teases a curl there between her fingers. 'So this is just for a little while, then...'

'I guess.'

'I'm not doing shit for my folks. I don't even call them. I probably should.'

I shrug.

I want to go back to her room. I think she wants me to come back too. She doesn't seem to care about this conversation; it's a placeholder.

'That's real nice,' she says.

In a split second, I fantasise about the two of us together in her bed, the afternoon sun bright behind the curtains and my hands on her and her mouth open and –

This bullshit with Jesse cuts straight through it.

I've got to keep moving.

'Sam, I've got to go.'

Gatton in September:

I drive into the heat.

I go to Coles and buy bananas and Neenish tarts.

I withdraw cash.

The wind blows dust through the car park.

There's no sign of Craig or the girl at his place. I pace around the outside of his house. The green plastic chair Craig mentioned is still sitting there in the centre of the yard. One of its legs has crumpled down and melted. Looks like Craig was almost sitting in the fire pit when we spoke on the phone. I spray the smouldering ashes with the garden hose, dump the tarts and bananas at the front door and leave.

The food science keg is a regular thing. I go, I tap the keg and I pour a few drinks. Then I try to talk to people and as the night progresses, I sell my weed to whoever is running low. It's been a good source of clients this year. The right kind of clients too. The foodies are all clueless fucks when it comes to Gatton. They live in a bubble, confined to Shelton Hall and a cluster of share houses near the lake. So there's not a lot of competition for their business. They don't seem to like other people. It suits me fine.

This afternoon, their party is starting slow.

I'm not. I sip my fifth beer before the sun goes down. Drinking this fast is not my strong suit but I need to keep my hands busy. My nerves are getting frayed. Jesse's not big on the foodies – *They're fucking mongs, man* – but he lives nearby and he occasionally pops in to check on me. That's what I'm hoping on.

Across the yard today, a band is setting up, laying out cabling on a broken concrete pad at the rear of the house. Beside them, a group of guys lay out a selection of catering, each of them meticulously setting it in lines like it's homework. 'Fade Into You' drifts out of the windows overhead.

I walk to the back fence with my beer and look out at the quiet roadway there.

I breathe.

This week.

And then it happens:

It's like I feel her closing in before I hear her voice.

'Nate?'

Chloe. My ex-girlfriend. I don't turn around.

'What are you doing here?' I say.

'It's nice to see you too.'

'Sorry. I just…'

'It's Joan's birthday. She wanted to come.'

I turn around and there she is.

Her face. Her actual face.

'What happened to you?' she says.

'Got into it with Pinchy the other night. How's things?'

'Under control, I think.'

She graduates in December and already has two days a week in a government place in Brisbane. She doesn't spend a lot of time on campus now. I haven't seen her in weeks and we haven't spoken since the break-up. That was July.

'How's your folks?' she says.

'Getting there.'

'Yours?'

She laughs. 'Do you really want to know?'

'No.'

'They're the same,' she says. 'How's Jesse?'

'Good, I think. I haven't seen him in a few days.'

'And you're okay?'

'I'm fine.'

'That's good, Nate. Okay, I might go and find Joan. She's inside somewhere.'

'Sure.'

And then she leaves. I want to watch her walk back to the house, but I don't. I turn back to the road and stare out, wanting to dredge up memories, but I don't let that happen either. I push her from my mind. Chloe saw some of this trouble coming. It's why we split. And now she's in her parallel universe and I'm stuck in mine.

I go back to the keg and pour another drink. I push it down my throat. My nerves twitch. My vision crowds. Not sure what this is. I'm thinking too fast and the booze isn't tampering it down:

Chloe.
Jesse.
Iris.
Maya Kibby.
The dog with her arm.
Dennis.
Hatch.
The rifle.
The money.
The weed drought.
The thing with Dad.
The thing with Mum.
Everything with my brother.
Chloe.
Chloe.
Chloe.
Her actual face.
And my assignments.
Uni.
Summer.
Eviction.

The world tilts. I put my hands on the keg to steady myself.

A voice says, 'Whoa, are you okay, man?'

Another says, 'He's fine.'

I recognise the second one. I turn around and it's Craig.

'Starting early, my man,' he says. 'I like it!'

I shake my head. 'Everything's fucked up.'

'Noooo, Nate. Nooo. Come with me.' He takes me by the hand down the side of the house, along a narrow little corridor there and out across the road to his van, a dirty white Toyota. He slides the side-door open and says, 'Get in.'

I do it. The whole cabin wobbles. He has curtains for the back so the inside is dark. There are blankets on the floor. Loose tools scattered around. An empty milk crate. An old street directory. Porn magazines stacked in a neat pile. A blue and white plastic esky sits on the floor, leaking water. There are three beanbags in the cabin and I plant myself in one, relieved to be off my feet. Craig holds up a small canvas bag and starts fossicking around in it.

'I'm still high as fuck from that fucking cake,' he says. 'I tell you, we're gonna make some gooooood money from that stuff. This drought could be good for me and you. Real good. Real, real good.'

The interior of the van feels too quiet and still.

'Here, you look fucked up already, so just have a little taste.' He opens a piece of baking foil and there's a row of small chocolate brownies inside.

'No man, I'm kinda freaking out. I'm...'

'What?' he says.

'I've got a lot going on.'

'We all do. But you look fucking tired, my man. Just have a little piece. It'll cool you out. You look like you need to chill. I saw Chloe on my way in. Who'd have thought that bitch would be at this thing. So weird.'

'It's okay,' I say, and I sound terrible, even to myself, like I'm about to cry. 'She's okay. It's not that bad,' and as I'm saying it, I'm reaching out for the space cake anyway.

'Just chill.'

It tastes pretty good, like cooking chocolate mixed with how weed smells.

'See, not bad, right?' he says.

Craig swallows a piece too.

I lay back into the beanbag.

Craig opens the esky and pulls out two beers. 'Here,' he says. 'Good as gold.' As we start on the tins, Craig digs out a little transistor radio and turns it on. He moves the dial, studying the thing carefully. 'You mind if I play the cricket?'

'I don't care.'

And so it is that we sit there and wait for the cake to kick in. I remember that I haven't slept much so I close my eyes. I nuzzle my head back and listen to the scrunching sound of the styrofoam balls in the bag and to the screech of the cricket call – the sound of the bat and the ball and the crowd's applause – and all of it starts to sound like static. I unclasp my hands and slowly black out.

I t's dark.
     I have no idea where I am.

The ground beneath me is warm and has a weird texture. It's humid too, the air hotter than it should be. I move my head and there's sound.

Crunch, crunch, crunch.

I sit up and reach around, finding a hard little bench on the ground. It doesn't feel like soil or rock. It has a plastic coat to it. I follow the bench with my hands to a cold steel wall, something familiar about it.

There's a latch.

I yank on it and the wall moves.

The van.

I'm still in Craig's van.

I step out and the sidewalk rises up fast. Without understanding it, I find myself lying in the grass. A night sky overhead. Houses on the edge of my vision. They're different. This isn't where I got into the van.

After a time, I find I can walk, so I make my way to the end of the street and look at the sign there. *Hennessy Road.* Down a way, I see the golf course and realise where I am. Not far from home.

I cut through the golf course and about halfway in, I see the showgrounds. I'm still trashed so I walk that way, crossing Woodlands Road and into Yates Street and from there I cut down a cul-de-sac called Goltz where Jesse lives. It takes a while but I find his place in the dark, one unlit house in amongst the others, no streetlights.

I go in and check the doors. I kick the screen a little. No one answers.

I do the same to the rest of the house, circling around, knocking on windows, whispering – or at least I think I'm whispering – *Jesse, come on! What the fuck? Jesse* –

The house is still locked tight. Every part of it.

And because I'm angry –

And because I'm tired –

And because I'm mashed –

And because of Iris and –

I pick up a loose house brick and throw it through one of the back windows and wait for something to happen.

Fuck-all happens.

No one moves inside. The house stays unlit. The neighbours' house stays quiet. All I can hear is the soft roar of the highway drifting in on the breeze. So I lay down in Jesse's yard for a while and stare back up at the stars.

I guess I pass out because it feels different, or later – or earlier – when I open my eyes again, it's still dark.

And everything's still where I left it.

The back window's still broken.

I go to the window and look at the damage. I've done a pretty good job of destroying it. The whole pane is smashed apart. Some of it sits on the floor inside. The rest is in two jagged pieces at my feet. Cold air blasts out of the hole. The air-con running hard.

Fuck it.

I need a drink.

I climb through into Jesse's office. I've been here a hundred times. It's the same room. Grim, not a lot of furniture. I go through and use his bathroom, piss in his toilet, splash water from his sink onto my face. There's blood in the water and I realise I've nicked two of my fingers climbing in. I wrap them in toilet paper and go out to the kitchen where I take a beer from the fridge. Despite all common sense, I open it and take a sip.

The house is like the cold room at work. It's fucking baltic. The remote for the air-con sits on the kitchen bench and I fumble around with it until I shut the thing down.

Silence.

Something's wrong.

There's something else in the cold air, something overpowering the overdue garbage and dishes, something worse than usual.

I feel like I'm being watched.

I sip the beer and check the rooms, turning lights on and off, trying to push down my paranoia.

The bedroom is clear.

The bathroom is clear.

The office is still clear.

The laundry is empty.

I walk back out to the living room by the kitchen and look around.

I hit the lights.

Jesse's there.

He's sitting in the corner staring at me. Except there's blood and foam leaking from his mouth and his face looks grey and bloated. His eyes bulge out like a demon, or a corpse.

When my brother Ray died, he had a car. A bright red BMW, less than a year old. He'd spent the rest of his money. After he died, my parents sold the car and used the proceeds to pay for me to spend my first year in the halls of residence in Gatton. My father insisted. He gave me that first year to get myself on track. 'It was what Ray would have wanted,' he said, which was a lie.

We should have saved the money. The halls were a nightmare. They were filled to the brim with ex-boarding school kids from regional Queensland. They all seemed to know each other, and they all – almost instinctually – hated me from the outset. There was no organised hazing but the proximity was punishing enough. I was privy to their lives, surrounded by them in fact. They seemed to drink all day and night. And their parties involved bizarre rituals and lots of fighting. For reasons I'll never understand, they bonded over physical violence against the hall's bathrooms: ripping off doors, clogging showers, smashing open toilets. My coming and going could also incite that violence. That's who I was to them: part of the furnishings. For the first few weeks of semester, I'd often find myself pushed up against a wall somewhere, for the grievous crime of coming past with a towel and toiletries or with my things for a lecture. It felt strange more than frightening. I didn't understand these people. I didn't want to.

That's when I met Jesse.

He moved into an empty room across the hallway from me about three weeks into semester one. I don't know where he was before that or why he was late to university, but from his first day on campus, things improved for me.

I can still remember it.

It was a Thursday morning. I was slipping out for my early Accounting tutorial and there he was, standing in the hallway in a black bathrobe, wearing sunglasses inside. He had an unlit cigarette draped from his lips.

'Hey, man,' he said. He put his hand out.

I shifted my books around, shook his hand. 'Hey.' I glanced around, thinking this was a prank or trouble. It had been a wild week already. I'd met Pinchy for the first time only a few days earlier.

'I'm Jesse.'

'Nate.'

'Nathan or Nathaniel.'

'Nathan.'

'Good call, Nate. Jesus, this place is. . . interesting, huh?'

'Yeah, look, I've got to get to –'

'I don't know anyone around here. You know anyone?'

I shook my head.

'You from Brisbane?' he said.

'Yeah.'

'I moved in last night. It was like a rodeo in here. Is it always like that? It was like something out of. . . '

'Yeah.'

'I actually saw a kid with a banjo.'

'Benny.'

'Benny?'

'He learned to play in the army,' I said.

'Jesus. What are you studying?'

'Business.'

'Same. Maybe I'll see you...' and Jesse trailed off as we both spotted a group of rugby guys approaching.

It took them a moment to see us. It was hard to tell with the sunglasses but Jesse didn't seem worried.

The rugby jocks started laughing as they got closer.

'What the fuck is this?' said the first one.

They all laughed louder, forcing it out.

'Is Riddell always this fucking gay?' said another.

'Gents,' said Jesse.

'What?'

'Good morning, gents, how are we today?'

'What the –'

'Hang on,' said Jesse. 'Do any of you have a lighter? I just ducked back in for mine. Can't bloody find it. I'm dying for a darb.'

'What are you wearing?' said one of them.

They seemed completely confused by him. I was invisible.

Jesse looked down at his robe. 'This? Who gives a fuck. Gents, let me ask you a question. Can I?'

'What, faggot?'

'Pffft, come on now. I was about to ask if any of you get high?'

They looked at each other. They looked at us.

'Yeah,' said one of them.

That was how we got through first year in the halls.

SATURDAY

I wake up vomiting.

No memory of getting home.

No memory of going to bed or the sleeping tablets.

I can't even remember coming out here to the grass and gravel beside the caravan.

Dawn.

Jesse's bulging corpse eyes.

Dark foam in his mouth.

I hurl again.

Call Iris.

But instead, my body lowers itself involuntarily. As soon as my head touches the ground, the world evaporates.

Hours later, and the classroom around me feels like a train roaring through a tunnel. Marketing for Business 2. My grip on the desk is so tight my knuckles are whitening.

A girl two seats along notices. Her face tells me a lot. It's like a mirror. She looks scared.

I loosen my hands and try to smile.

She looks worse.

I can still feel Craig's space cake running through me, just tinges of it on my periphery, out where everyone else is. I'm only here in class because I don't know what else to do. It's a mistake. I haven't showered or eaten. I haven't got anything with me, no papers or pens. I'm just sitting here.

And my friend is dead.

Maybe it's not real.

I follow that line of thinking for the hundredth time.

And if it is real?

I should call the police. I know I should.

I mentally rehearse it:

'There's a dead body at 23 Goltz Street.'

Then hang up.

Twenty seconds, tops.

Maybe more than twenty seconds. If they have to punch me through to someone, a detective or something.

No.

They're fucking cops. They're all pigs. They all talk to each other and they're all in on it together. That's how they get over.

The girl in my row looks back over at me.

'What?' I say. I think I might be mumbling.

She turns back to the lecture.

Maybe it's not real?

You had how many drinks last night?

And you had that fucking cake.

On top of the fact that you haven't slept in days.

Don't call the cops.

Check for yourself.

If the cops kick in Jesse's door, we could all land in it. Who knows what he's left out.

Check the house.

Check the house.

Are you fucking dumb? Check the house.

Your fingerprints are everywhere. Your blood is in his bathroom sink.

But I don't want to go back there.

I try to listen to the lecturer instead.

'–And then the customers move back to the start and

they bring back new purchasing behaviours with them and their –'

There's something else.

Another motivation, right back in the furthest part of my brain, playing like a song I can't remember the name of. Another reason.

Dennis and Hatch.

Money.

Their gear.

Fucking check the house, idiot.

I look at my busted hands and stifle a yelp. I bolt upright and stand there in the lecture hall. I can feel everyone's eyes on me.

Run.

I apologise all the way along my row as I brush past people, knocking their stuff around. I keep my eyes down.

'Sorry.'

'Sorry.'

'Sorry.'

'Sorry.'

'Christ, sorry.'

'Sorr–'

Jesse's house looks the same from the road. Another ordinary brick and tile place in a street full of them. There are grey clouds in the sky but the glare remains sharp. Cicadas drone in the trees nearby. This is the stillness of the flat country, paved over. No amount of suburban development can quite block it out. These streets will never feel anything but empty.

I go to Jesse's door and knock and there's no answer.

I go to the side fence and unlatch the gate – *How did I get this done last night?* – and the yard's there, and the clothesline and the peg basket and the hole in the rear window.

I go closer to the window and my stomach churns.

The smell.

My eyes water.

I climb inside, covering my mouth and nose with the crook of my arm. I head straight to the living room but stop myself a little way down the hall.

I can see his legs and feet from here.

Leather boat shoes.

Jesse's shoes.

It's enough.

I turn around and go to his room. In the en suite, I use the basin and there, behind two closed doors, I can finally deal with it. 'You knew he was dead all along,'

I whisper to my reflection because it's suddenly true. 'Nut up. Why are you here?'

I know the answer:

I'm desperate.

I'm here for his drugs and money.

I'm here to clean up before the pigs find him.

I'm here to save my own arse.

I check the medicine cabinet. There's a row of meds. I don't know any of the names until I get to the Alprazolam, which I recognise from my mother's stash. It's generic Xanax. I punch out a tab and swallow it.

I look at the rest of his things:

Condoms.

Lube.

Shaving gel.

And Vicks VapoRub. I take that out and dab some of it in my nostrils. It burns like hell but it blocks the smell.

I open the en suite door and move quickly for the rest of it, running almost. I know where he keeps his things. The cash is still there in a plastic ice-cream container under his bed. But down on my hands and knees, I find something else: a suitcase.

I pull it out and open it.

Videotapes.

Why does he have this?

There's something off about it. I flip it shut, pick it up and keep moving.

Jesse keeps his weed supply in the closet, in a backpack. There's not much left. Half an ounce of bud and two ounces of leaf. Jesse's main supply chain opens up in a lucerne field an hour's drive from here. An old bikie in a refrigerated truck drives it in. Money changes hands and the bikie hands over the gear in sealed boxes. This backpack is just his private stash.

What else?

He doesn't own a gun.

He doesn't own a computer.

I have his drugs.

I have his money.

I have his weird suitcase.

Time to go.

I wipe my prints off everything I can think of, then close the door to Jesse's office, the one with the busted window, before heading back to the kitchen bench. The remote's still sitting there. I look at it. I pick it up, turn the air-con back on and wipe the remote.

Then straight to the front door.

But –

I can't help it, I look at him one last time. Flies have found their way inside overnight and dozens of them now crawl across his face.

Jesse's dead.

Really, really dead.

I stifle a sob.

There's a knitted blanket on the sofa. I take it and cover him up, avoiding the bulging eyes as much as possible but not entirely. There's no peace in it. No grace either. Jesse's body doesn't look relaxed. He looks ridiculous. Like a dead guy sitting in the corner with a blanket over his head. The whole thing feels wrong.

It *is* wrong.

I open the front door and walk away. The rest of the street still has no idea. It's still quiet. It's still empty. The heat, the highway, the brown lawns, the bright summer light. Just another day in Gatton.

I pull off the highway and drive down a gravel track between two pieces of dry scrub, then park the car in the shade. There's no one out here but me.

I go to the boot and sort through the things I've stolen.

I sort the weed.

I could get a grand for it, maybe one and a half with demand this high.

I open the plastic ice-cream container of Jesse's money.

I count it.

Four grand and change. Not enough.

I do the maths in my head. If I close my bank account and sell everything I own – my car, my textbooks, my pager, my stereo and my clothes – I might scrape together four or five K, absolute maximum. Best case: eleven thousand dollars.

That's over thirty thousand dollars short for Dennis and Hatch.

I'm fucked.

Desperate and not even really thinking about, I open Jesse's suitcase in the boot of my car and look at the videotapes. They're all blank, labelled with small initials drawn in Jesse's terrible handwriting.

KT

SF

GW

KE

There's one that's different. It's in a pink case, spine down. I slide it out and turn it over. *Ejacula: La Vampire*. A blonde woman with her tits out on the cover. On the back, there's inserts of blow jobs and cum shots.

He never told me he had this.

I open the case and it's empty. No tape.

Scratching around in the rest of the suitcase, I find a notebook filled with more of Jesse's handwriting. He's ruled up the pages in a way I recognise. It's a ledger. We did these in first year. He's good with numbers.

Was good.

But I never knew he kept records.

I turn the pages.

The transaction descriptions aren't spelled out but the amounts are huge. On the last page, dated a week back, the balance is almost three hundred thousand dollars.

I think about Dennis and Hatch.

'Try forty-five grand. Do you have forty-five grand on you?'

I scan the individual entries. The transaction amounts are all smaller. There's a lot of them. Almost daily.

I turn to the back of the notebook and look for an inventory but there isn't one.

Jesse obviously knew what he had.

I don't.

I'm out on this road alone.

Think.

He has that money tucked away somewhere. It won't be in a bank. The taxman would murder him. And he's careless with cash. He puts it places. Hides it.

It could be buried in his back yard.

And then the rest of it comes to me:

Forty-five to the bikies.

Two fifty-five plus eleven left over.

Two sixty-six to...

Jesse's balance wasn't the sort of money that changes normal people's lives forever but it was more than enough for a whole new start for me and mine. There would be risks attached, but there was plenty of that already. The police would find Jesse soon. His suppliers were already after me.

But:

Two hundred and sixty-six thousand dollars solved everything.

I could quit Maccas.

Quit dealing.

Get my parents out in front of that second mortgage.

Leave the caravan park.

I slam the boot closed and the car shakes.

I could buy a new car. One with a manual transmission.

I'm telling myself all this because the next thing I need to do is difficult.

I ris stands by the stove stirring a pot of boiling water. She doesn't own a kettle, claims she doesn't need one: 'You can boil water in a pot.' She watches the water bubble and says, 'What do you mean, *dead*?'

'He's dead, Ri.'

'How?'

'I don't know.'

'But you saw him? At the house?' She says this slowly, as if we're talking about something else.

'Yeah.'

'But... how?'

'I don't know.'

'Don't fucking say that. You saw him. Was he... what? What are you telling me?'

She's closer now. She stares into me. There are tears in her eyes.

The water boils.

'He was sitting in the corner. He wasn't bleeding. He had... stuff... coming out his mouth, like he choked, maybe. I don't know. It freaked me out.'

'It freaked you out? *It freaked you out!*'

She takes off down the hall.

The bathroom door slams shut.

I wait outside.

Her crying echoes around the tiles.

I slide down the wall, spooked now, getting hit by everything and feeling it properly at last.

My friend is dead.

And my other friend, Iris, who is usually so unflappable, is howling as she cries.

I hear her vomit in the toilet.

'Nate,' she says.

And I will myself to go in but I can't.

Not yet.

An hour later, I tell her the story but I leave things out. There's no suitcase or ledger. No two hundred and sixty-six thousand dollars. No Dennis or Hatch. Just the story of finding Jesse and needing to restock to keep my life together. It feels weird to lie to her. She's a lot better at lying than I am.

Iris holds her joint out in front of us: a long pale arm and a hand and smoke drifting out. We're both stoned, lying on her bed with the afternoon sun thermonuclear bright under the shades. Her room is sparse, as always. She hates clutter. There's a desk, a chair, a wardrobe, a bedside table, a book, a lamp. That's it.

'I've got to stop smoking weed,' she says.

Her room feels like a pause.

I reach out for the joint. I take a drag, exhale and watch the smoke float.

Iris puts her head on my chest. She murmurs. Her hair smells like pear and it's flailed out. Her legs are touching mine. I want to touch her back but it's just the stress. I don't really want her. I can't. It's not like that.

'You know...' I say.

Iris murmurs again.

I look down.

She has her eyes closed. She's asleep.

It's dark when I wake. Iris is standing over me, finally holding that cup of tea.

'How long have I been out?'

'A while,' she says. 'Figured you needed it.'

I rub my face.

Iris sits down on the bed beside me.

'This could get bad,' she says.

'I know. What are you going to do?'

'I don't know. If it gets too fucked up, I'm getting out of here. You should think about it too.'

'You mean, leave town?'

'Yeah. Run. You didn't kill Jesse. The rest of it is the sort of stuff that the cops won't bother with.'

'It's a good idea but what about school?'

'School? What about it?' says Iris. 'The cops are going to be everywhere and you're a drug dealer. Sooner or later, things are gonna circle back if you stick around.'

'I think they already are.'

I'm still half asleep. I don't mean to say it.

Iris looks at me. 'Has someone said something to you already? Have you told someone else?'

'No.'

'Nate?'

'No, no one. It's just all my fucking people calling me. They want their stuff.'

I'll get the money.

She doesn't need to know the rest.

It's going to be fine.

I can pull the rabbit out of the hat.

It's going to be okay.

'You've got to stay away from all that,' she says. 'The police are going to come to your van in the next couple of days. You've got to be ready for it. You need to get yourself straightened out. I know you're...' But she stops. She doesn't want to say *scared of the police* but we both know I am and neither of us want to retread why.

'Why are you leaving town?' I say.

'I'm not. It's just an option.'

'But why?'

'It's always an option.'

My mind races, trying to connect things.

'Ri, you're not... you don't know something I don't...'

'What?'

'About Jesse?'

'No... No.'

'Okay.'

I stand up.

Police.

Bikies.

Iris.

One thing at a time.

Find the money.

At least fucking try, dude.

Then run.

I'm not an idiot. I know why I'm doing this. It's because all that stuff people say, that money can't buy happiness and that money doesn't solve anything and that money is the root of all evil: that's all bullshit. I'm studying business. I know about money. Money's just a tool.

And I'm going to find it.

Then I'm going to fix all this.

And it's all going to be fine, for once.

I drink McDonald's coffee from a paper cup and pick at my fries. The highway sits out the window beside me. Jesse's notebook is on the table. I've read every part of it but only a few details jump out.

It's page after page of numbers with no clear description. The dates go back a few months. The amounts start out at as a trickle and build up. Whatever he was doing, it was profitable. His margins are high and his outgoings light:

Expenses

S

Postage

Tapes

By the look of it, S is a person. Those S amounts look like wages. They're larger, tens of thousands, and they're regular.

S

I don't like it.

That's got to be Sock.

He's unaccounted for, too.

I push down the rest of my coffee even though it's cold.

I check my watch.

7:54 p.m.

The library is still open.

In the car, I roll up a joint, taking my first puff as I wait for a break in the traffic.

The campus librarian leans back in his chair and looks at my red eyes and my suitcase and my dirty clothes.

'You sure? We're shutting in an hour.'

'I need to check something, for an assignment.'

I'm here because I don't own a television.

Or a VCR.

'Okay then,' he says. He turns to the computer on the desk and taps the space bar. His whole face pulls together as he squints at the screen. 'This new database they're running is slower than the booking book. They give us all this,' and he waves a hand at the computer, 'And god, it's not even working now. It's not working. You *sure* you just want this room?'

I don't know what that means. I nod.

'Okay then.' The librarian looks around, like someone might be watching, like it's not Saturday night and we're not dealing with an empty room in the library basement. 'Here,' he hands me the key. 'Be back at quarter to, we're closing on time tonight.'

The AV rooms are downstairs. They're little white spaces: concrete block cells with a table, chairs and a combined VCR and screen. I have the key to the first one but they're all empty. The whole basement floor is almost empty. A kid sits nearby, hunched over a textbook at a desk. He's got his walkman on. Further down by the periodicals, a girl paces back and forth reciting something to herself. Neither of them care what I'm doing. Neither of them notice me.

I go into my room. It's brutally cold inside, courtesy of a loud air-conditioning vent. I put the suitcase on the carpet by the door, out of sight, and look through it.

None of the videotapes have dates on them. Instead, they're in alphabetical order going off the first letter of each initial written on the side. Tapes marked *AH* beside *BK* beside *DL,* and so on.

I grab Jesse's ledger and open it to the first entry with corresponding initials:

5/3/94–*QF*–$188

The tape is there. I slip it out and put it into the video unit. There's headphones attached. I put them on.

I press play.

Jesse lays back on the bed, shirtless, and says, 'I dunno, man.' His voice has the slight drawl it gets when he's toasted. He looks at the camera. 'I hope this works.' Then he looks directly into the lens, his eyes steady. 'I hope you're recording. Are you recording? I hope so. Don't let me down.'

A girl steps into the room, blocking half the frame with her bare legs. She's wearing white cotton underwear and nothing else.

'Who were you talking to?'

'No one,' says Jesse, smiling. 'Myself.'

'You're so weird,' says the girl and she coughs out a laugh. She sways a little.

'Come here.'

The girl steps centre screen.

Jesse's hands appear around her arse. He slides her underwear off, his hands moving gently down. The girl lets out a slow deep breath as Jesse starts tonguing her. When she's done, which takes a while, she gets down on her knees and opens his jeans. She has long wavy brown hair. She's still facing away from the camera and Jesse notices this as she starts.

'Hold up.'

He shuffles back onto the bed and the scene is almost

*comical: his cock protruding from his boxers, his jeans
around his ankles. The girl follows him up onto the bed.
There's a flash of her face as he kisses her neck, then another
as his hand sweeps back her hair like a veil.*

I know her.

It's Pearl.

Pearl Edwards.

She's a girl Jesse kicked around with for a fortnight
after summer break. She studies agri-business and drives
a brand-new car. I don't know why I remember that.

I fast-forward through the rest of the tape and watch
them fuck and roll around, pausing occasionally to look
at Pearl's body. Jesse is rough with her. Pearl doesn't seem
to mind – she seems to like it, at times – but there's an
undercurrent to it. I've never been like this with someone.
As I watch, it gets more and more intense and it takes
a while, minutes, to get through on jog-shuttle. When
they're done, there are long, long scenes where nothing
much happens. After a time, I realise this is shot in Jesse's
house before he got some of his new things. The film
ends with Jesse stepping into frame, looking out of the
screen at me, smiling, and turning off the camera.

Black nothing.

I check my watch.

I grab another tape.

This one is marked *II*.

I push play.

It's the same deal except the tape is wound forward
to a particular moment and it's nothing I want to watch
in the library:

*Hanna Harrington, a second-year from Toowoomba, wipes
her mouth, then holds up a long stringy wad of come to the*

camera. The shot is shaky. Jesse's holding the camera. His cock butts into the bottom of the screen and Hanna reaches for it. He wipes it on her – his cock – right across her cheek and I have no idea why.

I can't decide if what I'm watching is impossibly intimate or kind of creepy.

What is this?

I shut it off.

The room falls quiet.

I'm hard, despite everything:

Jesse's grimy bedroom.

The police.

The bikies.

The money.

I walk out and into a disabled toilet by the stairs. Inside, I drop my things and immediately unzip my fly, moving quickly, standing over the sink. It only takes a few seconds and I come so fast and long that I feel like I want to cry. I don't. Because there in front of me is the bathroom mirror and my reflection. *Is this the real me?* I look like a zombie, my half-flaccid dick dripping on the tiles. Behind me, a suitcase full of amateur pornography sits propped against the door.

Outside, the kid at the desk with the walkman is looking at me. The girl down by periodicals is also there. She's stopped her pacing. She's facing this way. They're both staring.

I walk fast.

I return the key.

I say goodnight to the librarian.

'What?' he says.

But I'm already halfway to the exit.

A road called the Ring surrounds the campus and I drive along it, past the halls of residence and the car parks, and past the lakes and the student piggery, around to the gym and to the Morrison building and down through open fields to the highway. It's a clouded night and dark out. I hit the high beams and head for home.

Back at the caravan park, I pull into the gravel drive and my headlights map out parked cars, an old trailer and two motorbikes.

Two men stand beside the bikes, smoking.

Dennis and Hatch.

Hatch holds a hand up to shield his eyes.

I brake and the car slides. I push the transmission into reverse and swerve back onto the road. I don't get far before I hear the booming roar of motorcycle engines approaching. I need to find somewhere busy. The Coles. One of the pubs. I speed into Spencer Street and as it becomes the start of Gatton's retail strip, I scan around for people. A horn sounds beside me. Hatch is riding alongside my car. He waves me over. He stays there beside me until a red light appears, then drops back. There's two cars in front of us. We all come to a stop and I sit there at the intersection and watch them in the rear-view.

Dennis dismounts. He doesn't rush. He puts the

kickstand of his bike down and lumbers up to the driver's side window. He makes a little winding signal with his giant hand. I notice his tattoos for the first time: a crude spiral on the back of his hand, lettering on his fingers.

I open the window a fraction.

'More,' he says.

He straightens up and moves his leather vest aside, showing me the butt of a pistol tucked into the waistband of his jeans.

I roll the window down further.

'Now,' he says, as if he's about to say something, but instead he punches me through the window. The blow lands somewhere around my right eye but also seems to cover my nose and the upper part of my lip. My face burns. I can't think. He grabs me by the throat and slams my head into the headrest.

'When Hatch asks you to do something, do it, okay? Now pull the fuck over.'

I nod, my hands frantically trying to pry him loose from my throat.

He looks at me, dark eyes beaming.

He keeps ahold of me.

A car horn sounds in the distance.

He lets me go. I lunge forward, gasping for air.

'See you in a bit,' he says, and leaves.

The lights have turned but I'm so flustered I can't will myself to drive.

Hatch rides past.

More horns.

I slowly pull my foot from the brake.

Across the intersection, I pull over by a car dealership, keeping the busy intersection close by.

I kill the ignition.

Dennis gets off his bike. He laughs as he walks up beside the car. Hatch has kept on riding and is now some way down the street.

'Where's he going?' says Dennis. 'Come on out of there.'

We watch Hatch's tail-lights come on. He pulls a U-turn in the distance, revving the engine violently as he motors back. On arrival, Hatch dismounts fast, cursing as he catches a boot on some part of his bike. 'Goddamn. What the...' He throws his helmet down into the gutter and turns his attention to me. By way of a greeting, he punches me hard in the stomach.

'Wait,' I say.

He kicks me as I'm crumpled over, catching my open side. I feel the bitumen and gravel on my face before I realise I've fallen.

Dennis picks me up and Hatch starts in proper. He makes two fast jabs: one collects my mouth and the other grinds into my side. I think he tries to headbutt me next, grabbing the hair at the back of my head, but the blow lands on the side of my skull. The pain is dull and huge, and followed by a ripple of warm through my whole body. I feel confused, and like I'm about to piss myself, and all the while I'm jabbering. When it's done, Hatch grunts and Dennis drops me back onto the road.

'You think I like hanging around in your hick caravan park, fucker?' says Hatch. 'Look at me, fucker!'

I try to turn my head up to him. Blood creeps across my face.

'I've got things I need to do,' he says.

I don't know what to say. 'I'm...'

Dennis steps into view and says, 'Where's Jesse?'

'He's dead. Someone –'

'What?' says Hatch.

'He's dead. I saw… Go and look… yourselves. He's… he's dead.'

I lay my head back down on the road. It's still warm from the day's sun. Dennis and Hatch's boots are right there by my face. The boots disappear. Then the two of them talk in a low murmur.

Dennis comes back. He squats down so I can see him. 'Your friend fucked you up, kid. He's got a lot of our product and we either need it back, or we need the money he made selling it. Forty-five K, remember? I'll give you another day. You either get it or we'll kill you and then this will all be the other one's problem.'

'The girl,' says Hatch. 'And then we'll probably have to kill her too, if she can't get it. And that fat idiot. Sock. Him too. Fucking hell, this is a mess.'

'And that's how we'll work. We'll just go through everyone we can think of: your friends, her friends, your parents, her parents. All of this Sock character's people. Someone has to get us that money or that product. It's just business.'

I say, 'But –'

Dennis grabs me by the shirt and drags me in closer. 'S'not fucking fair, kid, but it's how it is.'

Something cold and hard is pressed against the top of my head.

'Feel that?'

It's Hatch.

'What's he say?'

'Better answer him,' says Dennis.

I nod. I wipe my mouth. I'm angry now. I swat the gun away with my hand.

One of them laughs. 'Now, now.'

Hatch points the gun back into my eye, right there on the street. Everything else disappears, fades out. The intersection, the men, the money, the gun. I stop shaking and I feel a weird type of calm. I touch my mouth again and look at the blood on my fingers.

'Two days,' I say.

'What?'

'Two days. I need two days. At least. I think Sock has the gear. That's what people are saying. And he's out of town.'

'Is that right?' says Hatch.

'You sure, kid?' says Dennis. 'Because once this extra time we're giving you has gone by, that'll be that. We're not lying to you. We don't like having conversations like this. It's easier just to take you out to the bush somewhere and shoot you. So if your friend's got it, like you say, you better go find him.'

'I just need –'

'Yeah, yeah,' says Hatch. 'Two days. We're going to hurt you if you make us wait for nothing.'

'Come on,' says Dennis.

They back up.

I lay down on the road and roll onto my side.

The bikes start up. One, then the other.

A minute later, while I'm still lying there, an old man appears. He stands over me.

'You okay, mate?'

He holds his hand out.

I don't take it.

'No,' I say. 'I'm not okay.'

None of us are.

I've never really had any friends. Iris isn't a friend. We grew up together. We didn't choose each other. We played in the yard as toddlers, washed in the same bath, had sleepovers and shared Christmases. I can't remember a time before her and Iris is pretty much the same way. She didn't have a lot of friends either. Boyfriends, yes, but no one else. No one close. We didn't need them.

She had an easier time of high school than me. In grade ten, she transitioned from the girl no one noticed to the hot girl who wasn't like the other hot girls. She was shorter, slighter, not blonde. Guys who scared both of us wanted to date her. She went with it, as any sane person would, and by senior year she was fairly popular. She got invited to things. After graduation, she had plans and people to see over the summer break. 'They're okay,' she'd say, as if these high-school people just filled the time. Meanwhile, I was pretty much the same person I was at the start of school, only older.

Jesse was the first guy I knew who had options but stuck around. He had such a way with people that he could have slipped in anywhere. Ag-jock, rugby-jock, horti-freak, business-douche, they all would have taken him. Even the Gatton locals seemed to like Jesse. We normally didn't even talk to them. The locals kept to their pubs, we kept to ours. Yet Jesse was the only person I met in Gatton who slept with someone from town. He drifted between all the camps and when he had time for himself, he spent it with me.

He was different.

I don't know what he saw in me. I never asked. But we never struggled to find something to do. We smoked drugs, mostly. Jesse hated getting high alone. But we also drank together, talked to girls, drove around in my car, watched movies, played pool. He did say once – while slobberingly drunk – that he liked how unfiltered he could be around me. He said he didn't have to pretend. He told me that I was a good person. Which is an explanation of sorts, or was, until I learned everything else about him.

He never mentioned the videos.

I met Chloe – my ex – over my first end-of-year break. The university was offering summer credit and things were bad for me at home. My mother had finally started her long-overdue mental breakdown, and Dad encouraged me to stay in Gatton. It's how I ended up in the caravan park. It was cheap, temporary accommodation – just for that summer – until I met my landlord, Graham, and he needed weed. I was selling a little by then and we struck a deal. Once the rent was free, I could never leave.

Chloe didn't live there. The whole thing with her ran parallel to my regular life. She was a farm girl. She rode a motorbike. On our weekends together, we took trips out into the long, dry plains west of Gatton and sat on hills overlooking cattle country. We swam in dams and slept in cheap rooms above pubs. It was paradise for a while.

I loved her, I think.

The mood changed a little when the others came back for semester one. Chloe hated Jesse. I don't know why. Common sense, probably. Iris hated Chloe: she claimed Chloe looked down on her. The whole thing didn't bind together too well, but it was fine: no one asked me to choose. I kept them all siloed off as best I could. I had to: Chloe didn't smoke pot or get drunk more than once a week. She studied. She called her parents. She kept her dorm room neat. As we started into week one, I thought we'd settle into some sort of compromise, some middle space between my friends and her life. But as the weeks passed, she had less and less time for me.

Iris and Jesse hooked up in March, a couple of weeks into the new semester. It was one of those things that seemed fated, in the back of my mind. It happened because it was always going to happen. Things travelled along like that for a while. I saw a bit of everyone. I was busy. I worked at school. I worked at McDonald's. I sold pot and built up my clientele. I made money. I got my parents' mortgage back within spitting distance of workable. I was busy.

As the Gatton winter came on and the semester ended, things with Chloe never really picked back up. She accused me of dealing ecstasy one day on the phone:

'Harvey Barrett told me you sold him pills.'

'What?'

'That's what he said.'

'That's not my thing.'

'But you do sell pot?'

We'd never talked about it openly. In that exact moment, after weeks of getting brushed off, that riled me up.

'Not everyone's looked after by their parents.'

'Really, Nate?'

And that was that, pretty much.

We saw each other one more time but I don't remember why. It was over, gone. We both felt it.

She dumped me on the phone a week later.

I spent the mid-semester holidays alone, by choice.

SUNDAY

I wake up in my car at dawn and start thinking about where I can buy a gun. There can't be another run-in with Dennis and Hatch like last night. I won't survive it. I'm parked out in a back road I barely remember driving down. It's Sunday. I look at my busted face in the rear-view: a thick black welt under my eye, dried blood around my mouth, hair pasted down with something. I also see the suitcase of pornography on the back seat. The suitcase worries me worse than my face, the bikies and the police. I can't put my finger on why. There's something off about it, something darker than the rest of all this.

My pager flashes unknown numbers.

I pack some of Jesse's weed into a short steel pipe and smoke it down. It does nothing. The interior of the car feels like a coffin. I zone out and a couple of seconds later I'm back thinking about a gun and Jesse's body and his money.

I breathe out.

I brush it all aside again, for the suitcase.

What's actually in the suitcase?

What else is in there?

'No,' I say.

Get the gun first.

***

I drive to 808 Archer Road. They call this place Casa del Gangbang. It's the agricultural student share house to end all share houses. It's a rundown dump on the edge of a long cattle yard abutting the river. This is the last place on earth I want to be.

A row of elastic-sided boots sit by the door. Empty XXXX Bitter cans are piled up on the verandah. A sign on the door reads *No Kooks*.

I knock.

It's early, by student standards. 10:15 a.m.

A girl answers. She's all kitted out in tan riding chaps, leather boots, a maroon Broncos polo. She's holding a plastic bowl with cereal in it.

'Yeah, what?'

'Is Pinchy around?'

'What? Really?'

'Yeah,' I say. 'Is he here?'

'I don't know, man. He's here but…'

She lets me in and it's a nightmare. Ag students passed out on every surface of the room. A dozen people in the living room alone: three of them – three huge hicks, each in underwear – sit upright asleep on the couch. The girl with the cereal doesn't seem to care. She walks through the bodies on the floor, kicking one girl in the thigh as she looks for open carpet to step onto. In the hallway off the lounge, the girl points to an open door up one end.

I approach. Someone's snoring. The room is light, sun pouring in through an open window. The bed's in the corner, two sleepers. Pinchy's passed out, face down on a bare mattress with his arm draped down the side, his hand resting in a red plastic bucket. Beside him is a girl I recognise from the other night. They're both naked bar a matching pair of light blue boxers, the girl swimming in hers. She's the one snoring. As I creep closer I watch her breasts rise and fall in time, then I cover my mouth as the stench of vomit and sweat overcomes me.

I nudge Pinchy on the shoulder.

He jerks awake immediately and sits up. His eyes dart around the room like birds are attacking him.

'Pinchy?'

'What?'

He isn't really seeing me.

'Pinchy, it's me. Nate.'

He spends another few seconds glancing around then collapses back onto the bed. He rubs his eyes, tilts his head my way. 'What the fuck are you doing here? And why are you in my room like some creepy fag?'

'Can we talk outside?'

'What? Your face, dude, it's –'

'Can we go outside?'

'No. What is this? What are you doing?'

I watch his hand close into a fist.

'I want to buy a gun.'

Pinchy tells me to go wait in the back yard. The day is already hot and still. Despite the carnage of the share house, the property it sits on is beautiful. Blue gum flats stretch out for miles, and down further, short trees and shrubs hug the bank of a river. Way off in the distance, the land builds up and gives way to greener country, a tall wooded area. I think about where we are, what roads I used to get here, and I shudder. That's where they found Maya's body.

Pinchy comes out. He's added a blue singlet and thongs and has a half-smoked cigarette in his mouth. He doesn't speak to me. Instead, he points me over to his ute where he rips back the rear canopy revealing a long steel box. Pinchy scrambles up into the ute's tray and squats down beside the box, fiddling with a padlock on the side. As he's sorting keys in his hand, he thinks of something and stops.

'You've got money, right? Cash?'

I nod.

'Show me.'

I open my wallet and take out a handful of Jesse's fifty-dollar notes.

'Okay. What do you want it for?'

'Protection.'

'Looks like you might need it.' Pinchy finds the key, slips it into the lock. He's about to take a gun out when he turns back and says, 'I didn't do that to you, did I?'

'What?'

'Your face? Last night was epic.'

'No.'

'Okay. Good. I was fucking drunk as hell last night. Look, if you want to scare someone, a replica is probably what you're after.'

Pinchy lifts a plastic shopping bag out of the box and takes three plastic handguns from inside. At a glance, they all look real. I pick one up. I've never handled a gun, but the replica feels too light. I know that's wrong.

'No. I need something else,' I say.

'Well, I can sell you a rifle. Do you know how to fire a rifle?'

'Don't I just... pull the trigger?'

'Do you know how to load it?'

I shake my head.

'Okay, okay. Let's... oh, okay, this.'

Pinchy reaches in and pulls out a stubby gun, not much longer than my forearm. It has two thick barrels and a mottled brown timber stock. As soon as I see this thing, I know.

'What is it?' I say

He looks at me like I'm an idiot.

'Sawn-off shotgun. A classic. If you really need to protect yourself and you don't know anything about guns, this is what you want. You just point it at the problem and pull the trigger.'

'Is it hard to load?'

He reaches down and takes a red cartridge from the box, then breaks the gun open. 'Pop two in, cock back the hammers and you're ready to go. Your mum could do it.'

'Can I fire it?'

'Here?'

'Yeah.'

'Fuck no. Wake the whole house up. I'll sell you a couple of boxes of ammo and you can take it down the road a bit and go crazy.'

Pinchy hands me the gun. I hold it in my hands, aimed down low with the stock pressed into my bicep. I've seen this in a movie.

Pinchy laughs. 'Be careful with that thing or you'll end up killing yourself. Now, that gun is a personal favourite of my mate's...' and Pinchy gives me the hard sell for a minute or so, something about pig hunting. I pay him what he wants. I'm in no position to haggle.

'Don't tell anyone about this,' I say as we walk back to the house.

'Same here,' says Pinchy. 'You get caught with that, you're on your own. The cops can bust you just for having it.'

I figured as much.

Pinchy stops at the back door and looks me over. I'm standing there behind his house with a gun and a box of ammo cradled in my arms. His eyes are empty. We've never spoken much before. But now, there's this strange collaboration.

I drive further out of town towards that green forest country where they found Maya Kibby. As the air starts to cool, I take a dirt road and wind the car through until I feel good and far from civilisation. Standing there in the road, I fire the gun at a tree stump, tearing a large chunk of bark from it. The booming sound it makes is immense. The forest goes silent. It scares me and I give up after that first go.

I call on Iris but she isn't home, and for reasons unknown to me, I swing by Jesse's house on the way back to the centre of town. This is pot-thinking. Jesse's street is L-shaped and I don't see the police cruiser around the corner till it's too late. They have the street blocked off. Squad cars parked in a huddle further down. White vans. Plainclothes cops and uniforms at work. I pull a slow U-turn and idle up to the beat cop standing guard, thinking this will look less suspicious.

'You live down here, sir?' says the cop coming towards me. He leans down and looks into the car. He's young, black cropped hair. Everything neatly pressed. A huge man. *Why do they all look like this?*

My gut constricts.

'Nah, I'm... there's a guy down here who's supposed to sell me... a textbook.'

'A textbook. Right,' says the cop.

I watch him take a big sniff of the car.

'A textbook?' he says, again.

'For school.'

I'm blazed. I've slept in the car. I know the car doesn't smell right.

'Been in a bit of a dust-up?' he says.

I barely hear him.

I stare at his badge – *Alex Sennett* – and think about the things in the trunk:

Suitcase full of christ-knows-what.

Drug ledger.

Both stolen from the deceased's house.

And a shotgun.

I feel cold. I want to shoot this man. It's a deep reflex.

'What?' I say.

It's all I can get out.

'Your face.'

'Oh. Just a fight at the pub. It's not as bad as it looks.'

'And you were here for what number?'

'Uh, thirteen.'

'Who lives in thirteen?'

'I... I don't know. It's from an ad, in the student centre. What happened down there?'

The cop turns and looks over his shoulder.

'Don't know yet. It's not in number thirteen though, so you better turn around and get going.'

He stands up and I'm left staring at his belt and all the tools there. He has a gun. It doesn't look like Pinchy's replica. I inch the car forward then back, then I drive away. As I push down on the accelerator, I watch the scene in the rear-view. The cop has his notebook out.

I fall over and slide down a grassy hill on my way up into campus. The suitcase spills open and the tapes spray out. It's Sunday and the place is empty but I freak out anyway, cursing and scrambling to pile everything back in. I break one of the latches on the case. For some reason, I start crying. I grab at the grass, pulling handfuls out and screaming into the earth underneath.

The librarian on duty is the same arsehole from the previous night. He looks through me, through my busted face and my clothes covered in grass clippings, and he says nothing. Somehow that feels worse.

'I need the key to the video room.'

He hands it over.

He doesn't bother with the logbook this time.

In the little room, the same white cell, I lay the suitcase open on the floor and look at the tapes. They're out of order now. I pick one up at random – *LC* – and push it into the video player.

Kristy Batton sits on Jesse's bed and looks ahead, smiling. I know her from O-Week. We both worked the bar at the toga party.

In Jesse's room, her lips move silently.

I lean over and turn up the volume on the set.

'— *And then Moroney's like, Give me a go and, oh man, that was pretty wild. Moroney usually sticks to booze. She didn't know what the hell was up. She spent most of the night splashing things with a hose in the back yard.*'

'*Where is she now?' says someone off-camera.*

Jesse's voice.

'*Sleeping it off. Has been all day. Besides, aren't I enough?*'

Kirsty runs a hand over her thigh, turning slightly. She's in cut-offs.

'*Of course,' says Jesse.*

He steps around and sits beside her on the bed. They both look ahead and smile, like they're peering out through a window at me. They're looking at the camera.

I fast-forward the rest. Part of me doesn't want to but I do it. There are no clues here but I feel like there's a chance they'll talk about what they're doing. They don't. They start fucking, they stop fucking. At one point, she puts one of Jesse's hands around her neck. It's weird. I pop another tape in. *KE*. I press play. I recognise her too: Jessica Dyer, from the other day in the dormitory. I let it run while I leaf through Jesse's ledger again.

I'm not sure I'm here for the right reasons.

I keep going.

The code in the ledger is pretty straightforward: he's moved the initials forward one letter in the alphabet. Kirsty Batton or KB becomes *LC*. *II* from the other night is Hanna Harrington. Jessica Dyer, on-screen at the moment, becomes *KE*. I go back and scan the transaction descriptions for Kirsty, for *LC*. She's marked in for May of this year, the 10th. That's a week after the toga party. A week after I met her. *Did Jesse meet her that night?* I remember slipping him drinks at the bar. I remember him standing there in his toga shaped from Voltron bed sheets. I scan across in the ledger and see that the outgoing amount next to Kirsty's coded initials is three hundred dollars. A fortnight later there's incoming amounts attributed to her. Lots of them. Thousands of dollars of revenue for this one tape.

Is he selling this stuff?

How?

Who would know how to duplicate videotapes?

I go back to the suitcase and look through the labels. I alphabetise them. I pop tapes into and out of the video player quickly, jotting down the names of the girls I know. It quickly becomes a cavalcade of human flesh, of bodily openings, fluids, murmurs, biology. There's a list coming together on my scrap of paper.

Sandra from Accounting 2.

Megan from Intro to Quantitative Studies.

Rhoda from the campus club.

Karen from McDonald's, a co-worker.

Liz, a local girl, dimly recalled from a keg party.

Brea from –

The door behind me jolts and I fly around.

I go over and open up.

Someone takes the stairs. The rest of the floor is empty, quiet but for the buzz of fluorescent bulbs overhead. I go back to the room and watch more. I recognise more of the women, more of the names. I scan through the remaining tapes fast, feeling so numb to it all that I pick up the one marked *JU* and am reaching for the television to insert it when I stop dead:

JU.

That becomes IT.

Iris Tessler.

I'm sitting there staring at the tape, so fixated on the ink and lines of her coded initials that I don't hear the voice immediately. It's soft, so barely there in the conversation happening on-screen in front of me, that I almost miss it. The screen plays some tape I can't remember putting on:

'– *My god. What are you doing?' says Tori from Pitt Hall.*
Jesse laughs.
They're both naked, sitting up in the bed.
The camera moves, shakes a little.
A voice says, 'Just, you know…'
The girl squeals.
Jesse jumps out of the bed and runs to the camera, grabbing ahold of it, spinning it around on the operator and in an instant the new voice and the owner become one.
A man.
He's standing there, blinking.
The camera jolts down to his grey marl sweatsuit pants and his erection and the hand pushed down there with it. Then it pans back to his bearded face and his seedy ratfuck eyes. For seconds the camera sits on this face, his blank, stupid baby face.
It's Sock.
'You got any more of those pills?' says Tori.
The camera follows Sock to a backpack on the ground. He pulls out a clear plastic bag and taps a couple out into his hand. The girl takes one. Sock takes one. And the camera shakes as one gets placed in Jesse's hand. He brings it up and out of frame.

I pop the tape. I check the ledger. It's recent: two months ago. It all goes back to Sock.

I pack all the tapes back into the suitcase except the *JU* tape, which I carry in my hand. With my head down, I leave the room, taking the stairs two at a time. Up on the ground floor, I walk around to the reception, along the aisles, past the librarian's desk and –

'Hey!'

I keep walking.

'Hey, wait.'

I'm nearly out of there, so close I can see the prick in the reflection of the sliding doors.

The librarian. He's coming up behind me.

I turn around.

The key. I search my pockets and hold it out as he reaches me.

'Here,' I say.

He ignores it.

'I want to show you something.'

'I'm in a bit of a –'

'What? A rush? To where, with your suitcase full of –'

'No, you –'

'Just come and look at this, will you? Come on.' He walks away quickly. When he notices I'm not following he says, 'Come with me, or I'll write you up. You can't watch porn in the library.'

His voice booms in the quiet room. I feel the skin on my face burn.

There's a new room down the far end of the building, a space they've been renovating off and on since last summer. The doors are closed. The librarian goes to them and slides a key into the lock.

'What is it?' I say. I'm struggling to think if I've ever seen anyone go in there.

Inside, there's a dark room full of computers, rows of them side by side.

'You know what this is?' he says.

'Another computer lab?'

I type up my assignments in a lab like this across campus. I've never really been a big computer guy. They confuse me, have done since primary school.

'It's the Internet,' says the librarian. 'You know what the Internet is?'

'It's like some big encyclopedia.' My mother read about it in the paper.

'Something like that.'

He ushers me in and closes the door behind us. 'Do you know what's on these computers?'

'No.'

'Porn,' he says. 'You see all this, it's all porn. Lots and lots of porn. There's other stuff, obviously, but there's more porn than you've ever seen in your entire life on here. A fucking encyclopedia of porn, every type, all of it in there. The idiots in IT have no idea. They don't even know what they've installed.'

'I don't get it.'

'These machines talk to thousands of other computers, like a giant conference call, except you can transfer files around as well. You can get anything on here. There are already little communities popping up, little message boards about bands and TV shows and gardening and christ knows what else.'

'And people are sending each other porn.'

'Thousands of photos. Hundreds of thousands. There's like, a million perverts like you in the world. Millions.'

'I'm not a pervert.'

'Sure, man, neither am I. Neither are any of the guys I let in here, out of hours… for a fee.'

'You let people…'

'For a fee. I'm on nightshift four nights a week. Twenty

gets you in for the whole week. You do whatever you like in here, short of rubbing one out. You can download it, print stuff off, whatever you like,' he says, and then looking at me, he adds, 'You can copy photos from the computer onto a disc.'

'I don't think so. This,' and I shake the suitcase, 'it isn't what you think it is. I'm... never mind.'

'Well, if you change your mind, here it is.'

'Okay.'

'And...'

'What?'

'The tour costs twenty.'

I pay him. I've still got my wallet open when I have the one good idea I've had all week. I hold up another twenty. 'There isn't a guy called Jesse in your club is there?'

'Jesse Koerstz?' he says, reaching for the note.

I nod.

'Yeah, he was a regular. More than a regular. Spent a lot of time in here. Haven't seen him in a bit. Why?'

I shrug. 'Is there any type of record of what he did on those things?'

'I... ergh... I guess. But... oh dude, I don't know.'

'I'll give you five hundred dollars to show me.'

The librarian nods, slowly. 'They all have seperate log-ins I make for them, so let me go get my notebook and I'll show you his browser history.'

I don't know what that means but I wait as he goes back out.

A room full of dark screens.

Jesse was using something called a Usenet newsgroup. According to the librarian, a newsgroup is like a bulletin board, but for email. I don't have an email address but I know what one is. These newsgroups send community messages to you, via email, and the librarian tells me there are groups for everything: weird music, Dungeons and Dragons, Bible study, cigar smoking, you name it. Jesse subscribed to newsgroups about porn. Lots and lots of porn. And these groups don't even try to hide what they are up to. The word *erotica* and and *amateur* and *vid* are right there in the group titles.

For another fifty dollars, the librarian gets me into a few of the newsgroup archives and it doesn't take long for the rest to tumble out.

There are catalogues online.

There is a username called *Jesse_1976*.

The careless fuck.

The titles in one catalog marry up with the initals in Jesse's ledger. And there are photos:

Pearl.

Hanna.

Jess.

Megan from Intro to Quantitative Studies.

Rhoda from the campus club.

Brea from –

JU

Iris's face – the size of a postage stamp – there on the screen.

My breath heavy in my chest.

There is an address: *Send well-concealed cash to...*

A post-office box in Toowoomba.

I tell the librarian to shut it off.

There's a payphone outside the library block.

I call Iris.

No answer.

I call Sock's house.

Nothing.

I call his pager, then I dig through my own pager and call his girlfriend Mandy.

She picks up.

'It's Nate. Has Sock shown up yet?'

'No,' she says, somehow wringing a long pissed-off whine out of a single word.

'Has he called?'

'Yes.'

'When?'

'What is this?'

'Christ, Mandy. Did he call or not?'

She hangs up.

I scream into the receiver. 'Fuck.'

I call her back.

'Where the hell is he or I'm coming over there. There's cops at Jesse's house, you know?'

'What? That's crazy.'

'The police are probably looking for Sock right now. I'm not joking.'

'You're full of shit.'

'Why do you think he's hiding?'

'He's not hiding. He's... in Toowoomba, arsehole. I told you that. Why do you have to drag me into this shit? Why are you –'

'Where in Toowoomba?'

'I don't know.'

'Where? Where did he call you from?'

She falls silent for a second. I can hear her hand muffling the phone. She's talking to someone.

'Mandy?'

'Yeah?'

'I think he's in trouble.'

'Why?'

'I think we're all in trouble. I just need to...'

She makes a sound then, like a whimper. 'Nate, he's all fucked up, okay. He can barely talk. He wasn't making any sense last night and I don't want him anywhere near... I just... He said not to tell anyone where he is.'

'You can tell me. Come on, Mandy.'

She breathes in and out. 'He said he was calling from the Mobil on the range and was staying near there. That's all he said. Nate, you better not –'

I hang up.

Send well-concealed cash to...

I know the Mobil. Everyone knows it. It's a late-night greasy spoon on the edge of Toowoomba, thirty minutes west of here. Toowoomba sits on a mountain and that Mobil service station is the last thing anyone sees before the big descent.

I'm standing at the petrol pump at the Gatton McDonald's, filling up my tank and staring out at the fading sun.

What am I doing?

I'm driving around with a suitcase and a secondhand gun and a ledger and a printout of my best friend's worst sins. I can feel the ache in my face through all the weed and the dozen Panadol I've popped. It's all a dull reminder. All on the surface.

I'm pumping petrol and I'm thinking:

The police are coming.

The bikies are coming.

Something else, too.

The pressure and grind of it is bearing down on me and I can feel myself cracking open a little. Terrible, terrible shit is starting to come out. It's swirling around in my head. All this stuff I don't want to think about. All this garbage about my family and my ex that seems to reach me every night. And all the stuff about Jesse and all these images of girls I actually know, and all these memories I thought were happy but are, in fact, just the start of something bad. Something really, really bad.

And the police *are* coming. It's real.

The fucking pigs.

My worst fear.

And the bikies are coming too. That's real as well.

I glance around. The service station, the people, their cars, the highway, it all constricts around me.

JU

Iris's face on a screen.

I can feel my chest heaving. I think I'm going to cry, just standing there at the bowser.

But I don't.

It all comes to me and then peaks and rolls back, back behind a part of my brain that hides things. A part of me that just carries on.

Don't call the fucking cops.

Find fucking Sock and find Jesse's money.

Get out from under Dennis and Hatch.

That's what it's all about.

I start repeating:

Save this.

Recover this.

Don't be a fucking loser.

I'm scattered and I'm coming down, so I'm not thinking straight, not entirely. This is my mother's side of me. And my brother's.

This chaos is their chaos.

They lived here.

They're calling me in.

They loved this.

They loved this more than me.

The pump clicks and gurgles.

Tank's full.

All the car headlights are on by the time I reach Toowoomba. They call this place the Garden City, but it's a town. They have a business district, dusty department stores, suburbia, fast food and cattle money, but not much else. There are no high-rises. No bridges or tunnels. What it does have in spades is a bad vibe. Toowoomba doesn't aspire to anything. It sits up on the crest of the Darling Downs like it's teetering and about to topple back down into the low-rent plains below.

Out the windscreen, the Mobil service station on the range comes into view. There's no sign of Sock's van (a clapped-out brown Nissan missing a rear window). I pull into the lot anyhow. The place is empty except for two cars parked up against the kiosk.

Inside, three teenagers stand around the counter. They stop talking as I come in. I go to the fridge and look at the drinks.

'Can we help you, mate?' says the kid behind the counter. The tone isn't friendly but he looks about fifteen so I don't care. He has a small soul patch under his bottom lip. His two mates are both grunge kids. One's in a flannelette shirt that hangs open at the front revealing a skeletal, white chest. The other one's pudgier, in sweatpants topped with a Nirvana T-shirt.

'I'm...' I say, pointing at the fridge. 'I'm just getting a

Coke.' I've had a few cones on the drive up. Just to chill me out.

I grab a can and take it up.

Nirvana-Shirt looks at me like I'm joking. His mate bops up and down a little, as if he has headphones in, but he doesn't. There's half a Yin and Yang tattoo there on his chest, peeking out behind the flannelette.

'Just this?' says the clerk.

'I need some papers. And a lighter.'

The clerk opens the till and swears under his breath. He looks up, 'I got no change. I can give you five dollars in ten-cent pieces, or... like, some mix of...' He rattles the change drawer.

'Just throw something in,' I say.

'How 'bout a Mars bar?' says Flannelette-Shirt.

'Sure.'

They all look at each other, surprised for some reason. The kid on clerk duty puts through the new order.

'It's quiet in here.'

The two on my side of the counter both laugh.

Nirvana-Shirt says, 'It's this dickhead's birthday, so he put the petrol price up twenty cents a litre so no one will come in.'

'I'm about to quit,' says the clerk.

'Right. I don't suppose any of you can hook me up with some gear?'

'Maybe,' says Flannelette-Shirt. 'What are you after?'

'Pills.'

Flannelette-Shirt screws up his face. 'Nah, man.' It's too exaggerated. He's lying.

'You've got weed?'

'Yeah.'

They all glance at each other.

'I'm up from Gatton. It's dry down there.'

'There's always weed up here,' says Flannelette-Shirt. 'You want weed?'

'What will a stick of bud put me back?'

The clerk stays inside but the other two take me to a car in the car park. Nirvana-Shirt reaches in through an open window and pops the glove box, withdrawing a canvas library bag. He opens the bag and takes out a stick of weed wrapped in tinfoil. He unwraps it for me. Twines of ochre red fibre are threaded through the bud. It's not our gear. I take a sniff anyway.

'Good, right?' says Flannelette-Shirt.

'Yeah.'

I hand over my money and right on time, as if unlocked by the cash in his hand, Nirvana-Shirt says, 'Come to think of it, there is a guy around with pills, if you're, you know, desperate?'

'You know where he's staying?'

'Nah.'

'Kind of a fat fuck,' says Flannelette-Shirt. 'He's a new guy. Kind of slimy. Can't miss him.'

'Hawaiian shirt?'

'Yeah. Real shady-looking cunt.'

'Yeah?'

Nirvana-Shirt jabs his arm. Toowoomba is full of heroin.

'I don't want that shit,' I say.

'He's not flogging it, man. He's got this *big* fucking bag of pills,' says Nirvana-Shirt and he slaps the other kid on the arm for confirmation.

'Yeah, yeah, it's massive.'

'Does he come in here?'

'Yeah, man. He's around. Everyone comes here.'

'What's he driving?'

The kids check with each other. Both shrug.

'I reckon he walks in,' says Flannelette-Shirt.

'Yeah, yeah. I've never seen him drive, hey. But shit, he's always got that bag on him. He paid Ben in there with some of it the other night. The shit he's got is pretty wild, man. I could barely talk.'

'Right,' I say. 'I've got to go. You see the guy, give me a call on my beeper.' I take my *Missing: Maya Kibby* flyer from my pocket and tear off a small part of it for my name and number. 'There's fifty bucks in it.'

The two of them look at the scrap of paper.

As I'm walking back to the car I hear one of them say it might be time for a smoke.

Sock doesn't have the best origin story. When we met him, he was living in a share house with some of Jesse's first off-campus customers. They had a place out in Forest Hill. It was a real disaster; *Lord of the Flies*–level stuff. They all lived on home brew, Tip Top white bread and Nintendo. And their attendance on campus was so bad that it was months – literally months – before anyone realised Sock wasn't enrolled. He was a local. He had, apparently, picked up a *Roommate Wanted* flyer off the floor of a fish and chip shop in town. When he moved in, no one asked him what he was studying. It was that kind of place.

The sock part comes from that share house. The story goes that they had a party and everyone was mashed and it ended up being a bunch of guys sitting around the kitchen table talking about jerking off. They were diving deep on it, getting specific. Sock, it came out, had a particular piece of clothing he jerked off into: a red sports sock. Everyone thought that was a big laugh, an unusual addition to a list that already included disposable kitchen wipes, the bathroom sink and – I've always found this disturbing – a bedroom wastepaper basket. Yet in that room, with those dudes, this red sock would never have become legend were it not for one uncomfortable detail: the laundry. Sock told his story and as the laughing died down and everyone took a sip of their drinks, one of them started to frown and shake his head. *I know that sock. I fucking know that sock! I hung it out on the line last week! It's always in the laundry! It's... You... you sick fuck!* Sock was never much for laundry. But every now and then he popped the one item he needed into the machine, usually when someone else had a load on. This is the type of guy he is. This is who I'm looking for.

The motel owner lowers his glasses a little.

'Christoph Constance? I think I'd remember a name like that.'

This is Sock's real name. We all know it.

I'm on my second motel. Three sit within walking distance of the Mobil petrol station. I figure Sock is holed up in one of them. He's hiding. Hopefully with Jesse's money.

'What about Sock?' I say.

The owner takes his glasses off this time. 'As in, the thing you put on your foot?'

'That's right.'

I thought checking the guest register was a long shot, but the other motel clerks didn't care at all. The first place had a little old biddy behind the desk, a cig wavering in her mouth. *Nah, kid, no one's checked into this dump in weeks.* This guy is the same. He seems happy for the distraction.

'No,' he says. 'No guests called Sock. Can I ask what this is about?'

'He's a friend.'

'I see. And why do you think he's here?'

I can't see any harm in telling him. 'Some kids at the servo saw him.'

'Okay.'

'They said he was walking around.'

'Well, I'd try the Great Range Motel up the road. It's off the main drag but it backs onto the petrol station. Stinks, apparently. That's how close it is.'

He's right. The entryway to the Great Range Motel is further round and tucked into a suburban street, but the property runs all the way up to the Mobil's back fence. I walk the place through. It's on a big residential block with narrow paths and gardens and a sprawl of bungalows. As if on cue, an early night wind comes up off the valley it carries the smell of petrol. I search for the right bungalow, check the angles and write down the number I want.

The clerk behind the desk looks like he could be a close relative of Nirvana-Shirt. They have the same greasy hair, the same glassy eyes. 'Unit Seventeen?' he says. 'I have Twelve and Ten open?'

'I want Seventeen.'

He looks too confused to argue. This seems like Sock's sort of place.

'Is there a Christoph Constance here?'

'Christoph? I don't think so. There's a Chris? I think there's a Chris. It could be a chick, though.'

'Chris Constance?'

'I dunno.'

'Can you check the books?'

'Nah, not allowed.'

I look at my watch.

6:43 p.m.

My face aches.

I'm tired. I figure I haven't slept for more than a few hours this week.

I can't.

Jesse's body.

The videos.

My bruises and cuts.

Iris.

It's all on permanent jog shuttle in my mind, background noise to everything else.

'Hey?'

I'm staring through the desk. I look down and there's a Great Range Motel branded pen in my hand. 'What?'

'You were zoning out. Just sign here.'

The clerk puts the room key on the table beside the ledger and starts into his usual spiel about parking and swimming in the pool after hours.

'. . . And if you take anything from the mini-bar, there's a surcharge on each –'

'Dude, I don't give a fuck.'

He looks at me.

I stare back.

I grab the key.

I leave.

The bungalow is a split-level: lounge and kitchen downstairs, bedrooms and bathroom up. It has the clean antiseptic feel of early '80s luxury, lots of white tile and carpet, and while it's clean, every room has a humid, sweated-in feel. I set up in a room with twin beds running parallel. I dump the suitcase and the gun and a Coles shopping bag of my things onto one mattress and lay down on the other. From across the room I can see the JU tape in with my stuff. I still have it separated out. I stare at the black cassette's casing and try to see into it. Iris is in that box. After a time, I feel my eyes start to close.

B *eep. Beep. Beep. Beep…*
     Total darkness.

I put my hand over and there's nothing there, just the edge of a bed that feels too small.

Beep. Beep. Beep. Beep…

My watch is flashing.

I don't know why.

Then I do.

I reach up:

Beep. Beep. Bee–

It's 10:01 p.m.

Sunday night in Toowoomba. The equivalent of 5:30 p.m. Friday everywhere else.

I get up and go out into it.

All the bungalows in the motel are dark except one with a family in it. Sock isn't down at the Mobil either. I share a joint with the kid behind the counter, Benjamin. It's still his birthday for another two hours. He still has the petrol prices jacked up. There's still no one there. He kicks the curb outside the kiosk with worn Doc Martens and rubs his red hair. 'I've got to move to Brisbane, man. I've got to do some stuff. So much stuff,' he says. I tell him to do it and let him finish the spliff. In return, he runs Toowoomba down for me and I make a new list –

another list – on the same Maya Kibby flyer. Back in the car, I throw the now tattered flyer on the dash. It's folded over and the bottom half of Maya Kibby's head is right there, face up.

The smile.

No eyes.

It feels like a bad sign.

I turn the thing over.

There's a café called Bona Amici downtown. I've been there before. They serve booze. Bands squeeze into the back corner. Tonight, four middle-aged men sit in the front window, all in black, all looking like the Velvet Underground gone to seed. Behind them, two waitstaff stand around bored behind the counter, both high-school age. Down the room, a group of students sit around two tables on their way to getting rowdy.

I buy a coffee and a slice of lasagna and wait.

People come and go. A young kid sets up an amplifier. He's got an acoustic guitar. He's so drunk he can barely stand up but he manages to push a few chords out of the guitar and tune it. When he's done he nods vacantly at one of the girls behind the counter. Soundcheck's over. The house music comes back on.

They have a bathroom out back, up a set of stairs and down a corridor. As I'm sitting in one of the cubicles, checking my pager, I hear running. The door to the next cubicle slams open. Someone grunts and the sound is followed by the familiar sloshing of vomit hitting toilet water. 'Christ,' says a male voice, coughing. I take a quick peek over the top. It's not Sock.

Back in the café, a new contingent of students have piled in. They don't look like Gatton kids. They're not like Jesse and I, or Sock. They're decked out in op-shop wear. The girls and guys dress the same: baggy business pants, ironic tourism tees ('Cairns Is Beautiful'), rodeo shirts, trainers, beaded jewellery. One of the girls has purple-wash curls. All the men are more athletic than my counterparts. There's an art school up here and I'm guessing that's what I'm looking at: art students.

I hang back and sip a beer on my own.

After a time, two of the students – a guy and a girl – go outside for a smoke. They're busy rolling their tobacco when I approach.

'Can I bum a light?'

The guy tucks his pouch under his arm, feels around for a lighter. He finds one and hands it over.

I spark up a joint. 'You know who's playing tonight?'

The girl watches me. Cagey.

The guy says, 'Charles.'

I take a deep toke on the joint and hold it out to the two of them. The guy's still working on his smoke but he watches the girl out of the corner of his eye. She grabs the J.

'I'm supposed to meet a friend here. This guy Sock from Gatton.'

The guy says, 'Dumpy with a beard?'

The girl nods. 'The guy with the pills.'

'You seen him tonight? He's supposed to be here.'

The guy takes the joint, has a blast then replaces it with his cigarette. 'I want to get some more of that stuff. You know him, yeah?'

'Yeah,' I say.

We stand there a moment. I let it settle.

'Is there anything else on tonight?'

The girl says, 'Some hardcore band is playing the Nasho. There's a studio party later.'

These are both on my list from Benjamin.

The girl asks me where I'm from.

'Gatton.'

The guy laughs.

They take me inside to meet their friends and we drink a few drinks quickly. Because I'm bored and stressing out and stoned and tipsy, I flirt with a girl sitting at our table and then we watch the band. At some point I realise it's been more than an hour with no sign of Sock, so I leave. The girl, the one from before – not the one I've been talking to inside – she's back on the street smoking when I come past.

She says, 'Your friend's in a pretty bad way.'

'I know.'

I walk to the car and I'm about to slot the keys into the ignition when I decide I'm already too drunk and high and that I've got good reason to avoid the cops. There's a street directory under the passenger seat and I look up the National Hotel. It's five minutes down the road.

I walk. The Toowoomba CBD is dead. The pubs are full but the streets are empty. There's an old brick clock tower that reads 11:50 p.m. The day's almost done and I feel lost in it.

I'm alone.

I feel like something bad is catching up with me.

Grief, maybe? Or fear. Is the shock of everything wearing off? Every atom of booze and weed feels heavy in my blood. I stop there in the street and stare up at the clock tower.

Fuck Jesse.

And fuck Sock.

But fuck me as well.

There's a payphone. I go to it and call Iris.

'Hello?' She sounds tired.

'It's Nate.'

'Where are you?'

'Toowoomba. Where were you? I've been trying to reach you for... I don't know. I thought you left.'

'I haven't been anywhere,' she says.

I'm talking to her but I'm still looking up at the clock tower. I can hear myself breathing hard into the mouthpiece, puffing almost.

'What are you doing, Nate?'

'I'm looking for Sock.'

'Why?'

'I don't know. I think him and Jesse were mixed up in something bad and it got Jesse killed.'

'Christ, Nate, of course him and Jesse were mixed up in something bad. You *know* Jesse. You *know* Sock. You know all of this.'

'No, no, I don't. There's other stuff...'

I take out my bag of weed and start to assemble a smoke.

'What are you going to do when you find Sock?' she says. 'What's he going to tell you?'

Where the money is.

'I don't know. Who killed our fucking friend? Something like that. He's lugging around a bag of pills apparently. Maybe he killed him, Iris. Maybe Sock did it.'

My hands are shaking. I struggle with the light. I still have the art student's lighter. The flint ignites.

'Are you sparking up?' says Iris. 'Jesus fuck, Nate. *What are you doing?* You're all fucked up, wondering around Toowoomba, looking for that dickhead and –'

'And, what?'

'You know,' she says, 'you're just like him.'

'Like Sock?'

'No,' says Iris. 'Your brother.'

And the line goes dead.

And the clock moves.
Click.
11:56 p.m.
Clack.
11:57 p.m.
Click.
11:58 p.m.
Clack.
11:59 p.m.
Any second now.
Any sec–

I do the thing I try not to do every day. I think about Ray.

*E*veryone liked my brother Ray, even his victims. He was that guy. The one people looked for in a room. Charm down to the bone. Everyone wanted his attention. It was like a drug. And like everyone else endowed with his gift – that sense of intrigue, that way with people – it came wrapped in a bouquet of self-loathing. He made other people love him with unknowing ease because he had to. There was nothing like that generated internally.

He was a lawyer.

Eleven years my senior.

He was going to solve all our family's problems.

Dad never made much of himself. Mum didn't work. It was all on Ray. It would be easy for Ray. All he had to do was live his life and patch up my parents' bad finances. That's it.

Instead, he fucked it all up. He made things worse.

He got distracted. Ray in his red BMW, waving. Ray with his new suits and expensive hair. Ray yelling into his car phone. And so on. He bought an apartment and girls and travel and kept loads of cash in his wallet. He slipped Mum and Dad pocket change, promising more when the big break arrived at the firm. It went on for years but it didn't stop Mum believing it. 'Ray'll get us out of Eagleby,' she'd say, always an hour after he'd sped back up the highway in his luxury sports car, leaving us in Eagleby. That was the power of my brother's charisma.

Ray started taking the harder stuff in his mid-twenties. He'd always smoked weed, had given me my first taste of it when I was thirteen. That was pretty standard where we're from. (Iris could hand-roll a joint by then.) But Ray wanted more and I could see why. On uppers, Ray was super-powered. A fucking golden god.

He started rising faster and faster through the law world. We saw him less.

He sent the same amount of money.

My mum continued looking up to him like he was the sun itself and he rang her just often enough to keep things moving that way. I don't know what Dad thought. Dad and I have always been close and I've often wondered if that's why. I've wondered if Dad could feel the nuclear blast coming with Ray, right from the start, utilising some sort of skill I failed to inherit. I think he saw through Ray. And unlike my mother – who was totally wiped out, totally eviscerated, when Ray died – Dad stayed upright. He lost a son and the only time I saw him teeter was one night, months later. He was drunk, sitting on the living room couch. It was just the two of us. Out of nowhere he said, 'What was I supposed to do?'

I didn't have an answer for him.

Even Ray couldn't deal with Ray.

One night, just before he died, Ray came home. He stayed in the room beside mine, his old bedroom. Something was wrong. He came in late and he looked like hell. After the house resettled – Ray in his old bed, Mum and Dad back in their bed, me in mine – I could hear him crying, through the wall.

Mum and Dad sent me round to Iris's place the next morning. I was fourteen years old but a young fourteen. I did whatever they told me to do. Apart from a bit of pot and

some underage drinking, I was still that kid who watched
Hey Hey It's Saturday *with his parents – in his pyjamas –*
at fourteen. I still didn't really know what the world
was like.

And I loved Ray.

I loved him, just like Mum.

So I snuck home that night – late – and crept into Ray's
room and he was still up, sitting in his old bed, smoking a
cigarette.

'Are you in trouble?'

He just stared ahead.

'Iris and I are gonna go down the creek tomorrow. You
wanna come?'

He smiled, a little.

That was the last thing I ever said to him.

The police came a couple of hours later. They kicked the
door in and punched Dad and pushed Mum into a wall
while three of them kicked Ray's bedroom door in and
dragged him off. I saw it all. I was asleep on the floor by his
bed. Ray screamed the whole time.

From there, the story goes that Ray resisted arrest,
that he struggled as they took him from the wagon to the
holding cell in the Beenleigh stationhouse. Apparently,
he clipped his head on the lip of something, a door or a
bench or something. In a weakened state – in withdrawals,
apparently – his body just shut down. They worked on him
but he died almost instantly.

They tried to keep the details of Ray's death from Iris and
me. They told us Ray died in an accident. A 'mistaken
identity' or some bullshit. It was Mum, mainly, and that lie
had a shelf life of about a month.

One night, a man came to the door and yelled at Dad.

I gleaned a few details. Someone's daughter was dead too, another lawyer. Ray was 'a shit-bag drug addict' and the man's daughter 'never went near the stuff before she met him.' I listened at the window, writing down whatever I could hear in a small spiral-bound notepad, like a journalist or a detective.

It became a project of sorts after that. I asked around. An older kid at school – the son of a teacher who taught Ray – he told me my brother deserved to die but wouldn't say more. He told me to ask my parents.

I asked Iris what she thought.

'Do you really want to know?' was her answer.

I did.

I was an idiot. I asked Mum. That ended with her locked in her room with Dad rushing home from work. Then lots more yelling. Dad slipped into my bedroom afterwards. I can still see his beard and sad eyes in the half-light of the reading lamp: 'An accident, Nate. That's all it was. We'll talk about it more when you're older. Your brother just got himself into trouble he couldn't get out of. That's all it was.'

That did nothing.

I rang the police the next day. My voice had broken and I sounded older than I was. I told them I was doing research on a relative. They couldn't help me but as the constable rang off, she mentioned the newspaper archive. 'It got written up,' she said.

The State Library had the papers. I made plans, set a date and looked up the train timetable. I put together a cover story for my parents: a late night of homework in the city.

The day before my big plan, an older girl came to my school. She was dressed in a pink sweatsuit, no make-up, bad hair. She was pacing back and forth as I walked out the school gate. 'You want to know what happened to your brother?' she said before anything else. 'Yeah, you. I know who you are, you're Nathan Byrne and Ray Byrne was your fucking brother. You know who I am? I'll tell you...' and she fished around in her handbag. The girl held out a photograph of a blonde woman in a university gown, smiling against a fake marble backdrop. 'This is my big sister. And your idiot brother killed her. Your fucking brother.'

I couldn't handle it. I pushed past her and started walking.

She followed. She kept shouting:

Something about bad drugs.

Something about a cockroach and a toilet.

Something about how my family would rot in hell.

Then she said a lot of stuff about how Ray – my brother in the next room, the person I loved more than my own mother, the older guy who spent most of his life talking to me like I was a real person, who never once lashed out at me or hurt me or let anyone do wrong by me, even in his worst moments –

She told me Ray deserved to die.

This was the second time I heard it.

And for some reason, it sank into me like stone. I believed her.

I was too young for any of this.

The next day, I skipped school and caught the train to the State Library. There, I went to the newspaper archives as planned and scanned the microfilm. The story was buried but I unburied it. Ray and two law clerks – a guy and a girl – all OD'd in the bathroom of a nightclub. During the night, Ray came to and ran. The other two died. The toilet was upstairs in some quiet VIP part of the nightclub. Their bodies lay there all night, the two of them slumped over each other. A detective constable interviewed by the paper said that they might have lived had someone found them sooner.

Further down, it said my brother – 'still at large' – bought the drugs from a man currently in custody for questioning.

That afternoon, I walked across the bridge and into Brisbane proper. The nightclub where the people died was down in the business district. I stood across the street from it and watched a few customers go in and out. None of it made much sense. Seeing it didn't change anything.

I caught the train back home in time for dinner.

A year later, the pigs who smashed up our house – who punched my father and pushed my mother, and dragged my kicking and screaming brother over the floor of the stationhouse until his head burst open – they got off. They're still cops. One of them works on the Gold Coast now. I don't know where the other one is.

It's weird. A cop killed a black guy up north in similar circumstances, on some island, and everyone came together and rioted. They burned the pig's house down.

That's what we should have done.

Instead, my parents took out a second mortgage and tried to sue the Queensland Police Service.

It didn't work. That court case ruined my parents.

Even a year later, someone was still spraying MURDERER on the front fence in red spray-paint. We cleaned it off, over and over again. One time, as we worked, Dad told me there were other people involved in Ray's accident.

I nodded along like I didn't know.

More lies.

It gets to be like poison in the blood.

People talked shit to me at school. It became something I never really recovered from, not socially. I was no one before. Now I was somehow less than that. It got too much for Iris.

That's when she started trading on her looks and hanging out with the popular kids.

On Ray's birthday, three years after he died, Dad came out into the living room and said, 'That's the end of that,' which was both true and untrue. Life kept happening. The fallout kept coming. Mum never recovered. Mum had a nervous breakdown. Mum went in and out of hospital. Dad lost his job, got another one, and lost that too. The bank started calling. It was monthly at first. Then the calls came faster, after I went to university to study business.

MONDAY

The clock over the bar at the National Hotel reads 12:44 a.m. It's a loud night. Punk-rock kids wall-to-wall, pouring in and out of the back room where the bands play. I sit at the bar and watch the bartenders load them up with drinks, turfing out the underage and stone drunk. There's no security. The guys behind the bar do all the manhandling themselves.

One tough old bastard is doing a lot of it. He's getting tired now.

'You can't be serious!' he shouts.

I turn around.

A kid is trying to come in. He's covered in vomit, face to waist, and he's so pissed that he's hanging onto the door jamb like there's a cyclone outside.

'I fucking told you, mate!'

The kid barely notices. He keeps pulling himself inside.

'Fuck! Fuck! Fuck!'

Two of them run over there.

I don't watch the rest.

These comatose kids are everywhere. This is Sock's handiwork. A girl two barstools down reckons she saw him. She had a lock on someone who looked just like him. *Charles Manson mixed with Al from* Home Improvement.

That was Sock. She said he'd mostly just sat by himself in a corner with a jug of beer.

I wait anyhow.

He doesn't reappear.

The old bartender serves me a beer, but he places a schooner of lukewarm tap water down beside it.

The studio party is the last thing on my list and it's a big ask. I shuffle up Russell Street, hoping I'm headed the right way. I smoke a joint and pray for clarity and a late-night convenience store, finding neither. I'm about to give up on everything when I come across a group of guys sitting with their feet in the gutter, beer cans spread out. One of them has a goon bag in hand.

I ask them if they've seen a fat guy with a beard and a bag full of ecstasy pills.

They laugh at that.

The guy with the goon bag offers me a lay-back.

'I'm fucking mashed,' I tell him. 'But thanks.'

'What happened to your face, man?'

'I fell over.'

Another voice says, 'Hey, hey, dude?' It's a big guy, sitting in the group's centre. He has sandy blond hair and a matched beard. 'Hey?' he says again.

'Yeah, man. What?'

'I've got something I want to ask you.'

'Yeah, what's that?'

'Just something. Just look at me. You ready?'

'Yeah.'

The earth's surface is tilting back and forth. It's hard to fix my eyes on him.

'Just look at me,' he says.

'What?'

I stare at his face, his eyes. I look at his dirty white

singlet – worn through with sweat despite the mountain chill. And I look at his shorts and that's when I see his balls proudly flopped out the leg of his rugby shorts. They're huge. Pale and sickly white, covered in that same blond hair.

'Jesus,' I say.

They all laugh and it lasts a minute or so. I'm flushed and don't want to leave without saying something more, so I ask if there's a store around. 'I need a sausage roll.'

'We're going to the Mobil, if you wanna come?' says one of them. It's the little guy on the end, the one with the goon bag. I look at the rest of them. They're all talking to each other, barely aware I'm still there.

'When are you going?'

'Me and this knob are going now,' says the kid. He struggles to his feet. 'Whoa.'

'Are you driving?'

'Nah, man.'

The kid and two of his mates take me over to a parked van and knock on the side. The rear door opens. There's a girl in there. She sits up, wiping her eyes.

'Are we going home?' she says.

The kid doesn't answer. Instead, he crawls in beside her and lies down. Then murmurs, 'Mobil.' The other guys get in the back but I go round to the passenger seat, feeling a bit suspicious. The girl crawls through and sits behind the wheel. As she struggles to slot the keys into the ignition, I ask her if she's been drinking.

'Not heaps,' she says. She stops and looks over. 'Do I know you?'

'I just met these guys tonight.'

'Right.'

The engine chokes and starts. The van shunts forward and we start out through the empty streets. The girl puts the stereo on and smoothly pushes through the van's gears. The music sounds familiar – female vocals, mid-tempo guitars – but I can't place it.

'What's this?'

'Ice,' she says.

We pass the café from before and drive out of the business district into the leafier inner suburbs. As we turn out onto the main artery running the edge of Toowoomba, we steer into a slight incline. Across the lane, a giant cattle truck bears down on us. The girl says something soft and lilting under her breath, something more about ice.

'What's that?'

She laughs. 'I was just... Damn, I hope I don't hit that.'

I get fast visions of steel grinding into steel and the van flipping onto its side, my window skating along the tarmac and spraying sparks.

The girl takes a hand off the wheel. She adjusts the rear-view mirror. She looks at herself.

The truck passes.

The whole van rocks in the slipstream.

I say, 'How high are you?'

'Not heaps,' says the girl. 'Why?'

'Buuuuulllshit,' says one of the guys in back.

'Okay. Pretty high, I guess,' says the girl. 'I'm fucking hungry. I know that much.'

I'm staring at her, mentally willing her not to kill us all as she eases the van to a standstill in the road. I turn around and a red light glows through the dirty windscreen. Nothing out there except a figure shuffling across the other side of the intersection.

'I really want a Chiko roll,' says the girl. 'I wonder where I can...'

I stop listening.

It's Sock.

Sock is the figure walking across the intersection.

I struggle with the seat belt.

'What are you doing?' says the girl.

'Sock!' I scream. 'Sock!'

He turns for a moment as I come out the van door. I'm not sure if he sees me or if he's just spooked by the screaming because he starts running. I chase after him. I'm out in the middle of the empty intersection when the van's horn sounds behind me.

'Shut the door, dude,' yells the girl.

I holler back that I'm sorry and, because I'm drunk, running down an open road in the middle of the night, I keep shouting.

'Wait, wait, wait, wait –'

Sock is about fifty metres ahead of me, his huge shoulders jiggling up and down comically as he runs.

I'm still saying it:

'– Wait, wait, wait, wait, wai–'

I catch my foot and trip, careening over into the grassy sidewalk. As soon as I hit the ground, I start rolling.

Sky.

Streetlight.

Dirt.

Sky.

Streetlight.

Grass.

When it's over, I pat my face and sit up.

An empty road.

'Fuck.'

I get up and start running again. There's a schoolyard on the left and I figure he's ducked in there. I jump the fence and dart between two buildings.

'Sock?'

A courtyard lined with buildings. I keep moving, figuring if I stop, I'll lose him. I cross over and run between more of the buildings, praying I don't trip again in the dark.

'Sock, it's me.'

A tree-lined corridor.

A tall brick wall.

No sound except my own breath.

I cut down a small passageway and find myself out in a sports field with the moon overhead.

I scream his name one more time.

'Sock!'

He's gone.

The motel.

My legs burn but I sprint anyhow. I flail my way up the hill towards the Great Range Motel and I'm close when I see Sock's van barrel out the driveway. He stalls it in the middle of the road and by the time he's got it restarted, I'm running alongside, banging on the rear panel. He puts his foot down and peels off, trailing thick toxic exhaust. He's headed east, down the range.

My first instinct is to drive after him.

But the suitcase, ledger, shotgun.

And my car? Where's my car?

I jog into the motel complex. None of the bungalows are lit except for an old couple watching TV, the flickering blue light on them. Out the back, down near my unit, I spot a wide-open door, a black invitation. The smell of hamburger grease and sour milk drifts out on a warm current of air.

'Sock?' I say, stepping in. I don't know why. I just saw him leave.

I fumble around in the dark, slotting some sort of

switch on the wall. The kitchen lights up. I squint around.

'Anyone here?'

The place is a wreck. Pizza boxes piled waist-high by the refrigerator. Every piece of kitchenware – every plate, pot and utensil – piled up around the sink. A frightening blood-red pool sits on the main counter, an upturned can of tomatoes at the centre. Beside the can lies a bag of unopened dried pasta.

I go through to the living room and check for signs of life. Sock's bungalow is identical to mine so I recognise the door off to the laundry, the stairs leading up to the bedrooms above, the salmon-coloured curtains and rough industrial-grade carpet.

'Anyone?'

I go upstairs. One bedroom is empty (a bed and an unrolled camp swag on the ground) but the other room is decked out with racks of electrical equipment. There are rows and rows – floor to ceiling – of white boxes. They look like VCRs; each has a slot the size and shape of a videotape. A small monitor sits on top but it's switched off. None of it is running. I take the stairs back down two at a time. On closer inspection, the lounge room isn't much better than the kitchen. More rubbish, more piles. A crumpled sleeping bag lays unsheathed on the couch. I go to the laundry. I gently nudge the door open with my foot. There's no one in there but there is a small en suite off the laundry, and in this room I learn first-hand how far Sock has fallen. A pile of used syringes sits by the toilet. Tufts of burnt tinfoil in a heap. The toilet bowl and floor tiles are caked in blood, shit and bile. I stare at it all and feel a rush of heat in my face. I turn and lunge for the laundry sink, beer gushing from my mouth, coming up so hard I can feel the spray rebounding back into my face.

***

I trash the place, take every piece of it apart looking for whatever Sock may be hiding. It doesn't take long. Sock's junk-brain is even worse than his regular head and I could have stopped after the first five minutes. He came back to the unit for his dope and he's out of his mind because at the end of my raid I have a bag of fifty white pills with rocket ships stamped on them (inside the couch), half an ounce of bud (pantry) and a long-blade hunting knife. There's leftover beer, as well. When I'm finished, I crack one open and stare at the living room and what's left of it. *What else did he take?* In my frenzy I almost forget the VCR player in the living room but it catches my eye on the way out. I push open the little compartment door on the machine and look inside. There's a tape.

Back in my bungalow, the world's falling apart. My door's locked. My blinds are drawn. I pace around, looking at the items on the coffee table:

Two fucking tapes now.

Iris or Sock.

I let out a sound I've never heard myself make before, some utterance halfway between a sob and a scream.

'Wash your face. Fuck. Cold water.'

I strip to the waist and soak a tea towel in the kitchen sink and wash myself down. There's blood, grass and dirt in the water. A clock ticks on the wall beside me.

4:35 a.m.

Fatigue is creeping in. Raw white pain throbs behind my eyes and my throat is dry and sharp.

I'm slowing down.

But I can't slow down.

I shotgun another tin of VB and it gives me two minutes of energy.

'Pick a tape, any tape,' I say. 'Any tape at all.'

Jesse's *JU* sex tape or Sock's untitled one.

Iris or Sock.

I'm getting weak.

I'm alone and tired and drunk and terrified and angry and sore and worried and confused and paranoid. No thought coheres to the next but I can feel something. It's not just the booze and weed talking. I know there's something else here. And I'm a piece of shit. And I need some sort of relief. I push the *JU* tape into the player and unbuckle my jeans and I'm crying before she even comes on screen.

Iris stands on the bed in her underwear. She grows larger in the frame. There's a rough zoom in to her breasts: two small almond-white mounds, the ridge of vivid pink nipples through the sheer. She cups herself and blows an exaggerated kiss.

The picture shunts and spins.

She laughs.

'I'm tripping all over myself to fuck you,' says a loud, familiar voice.

Jesse.

'Here,' he says.

More movement, then Jesse appears in tight jockeys. A foregrounded hand juts in and starts rubbing at his crotch. That's Iris's hand. His crotch, the profiled cock underneath, the hand, these fill the screen.

The frame goes haywire again.

Iris. Her face.

She looks up at him.

I'm an idiot. I can't even get it up for this. I buckle up my jeans, finding some deeply submerged store of dignity. I get another beer. I hit the fast-forward button.

Iris sucking Jesse eating out Iris fucking Jesse, on top from behind, underneath, and her hand jerking him until he...

Iris naked in careful detail then Jesse naked and the room spinning and then Jesse and Iris sucking, fucking, sweating, screaming, laughing, wrestling with the sheets stretched out like an alien landscape over and over again and endless until... another day and more of the same, different outfits but all the same things except more: more mouth, more cunt, more cock, more spit, more skin until... another day: another round... and another day: another round... it gets rough in places: Jesse's clear handprint on Iris's arse... and another day, in the car this time and half out of focus with jump cuts, edits and more passing days, weeks and hours. Iris and Jesse and the boring, endless fucking, sucking, fucking, spanking, fucking, sucking, fucking, coming, fucking, groaning, fucking, laughing, fucking, fucking, fucking and then, without any sort of introduction or build-up, in there amongst all the other pink openings and wet skin and pumping biology and the mouths and tongues and dicks, in amongst all that: there is another person, a woman, a threesome and the frame...

I hit play. The sound comes on, the moaning:

The new woman's skin is olive. She has black straight hair. It covers her face. Iris runs her hands over the woman's breasts, the woman's head cradled gently in Iris's naked lap. Jesse fucks the woman. The camera pans roughly between the point of connection – a grisly, unglamorous thrusting – and back to the woman and Iris at the other end. Screaming, Jesse yanks his cock out and sprays over the woman's belly and when he does, the new woman lifts her head to look and her face...

I hit pause.

I am sober, instantly.

I stare at the screen for minutes. Her face is huge; twice the size and like a ghost.

I get up and move closer to the screen. I feel the static sizzle of my pores near the glass.

I know her.

Everyone knows her.

I've been carrying around her picture.

Maya Kibby.

The dead girl.

I hit eject and put the other tape in.

It's worse.

It's short: ten minutes.

It's related.

It's the end of everything.

Halfway down the range I come back to myself and panic. I steer the car off the road into an emergency stopping lane, gravel ricocheting along the undercarriage, swerving to a halt. An eerie stillness washes over me as I sit there and listen to the tiny echoes of the scrub.

I don't remember leaving the motel.

I don't remember walking back to the car.

My hands are locked around the wheel. I pry them loose and go check the boot.

The gun is there.

The suitcase.

My bag. I open it. I reach inside and breathe out a lungful of air as I realise that Sock's bag of pills is still in there and his ounce of pot as well.

I can't see the hunting knife anywhere. I don't know what I did with that.

I look at the open boot and think.

Sock's tape.

I stand there in the dark and try to ease my mind over parts of it without seeing the whole thing:

Jesse and Maya sprawled out on the bed. Her hands on his face. He's not even really looking at her.

There's a shitty little town called Withcott at the bottom of the mountain range. The service station there is closed – the whole township is dark except for the bakery – and there's a phone booth. I call Iris. As I listen to the call ring through, I lay my head against the window glass and close my eyes.

A motorbike roars past on the highway, just a flash of light and sound.

I open my eyes, dial tone in my ear.

Asleep standing up.

No answer.

I go back to the car and take the pills out of the boot. I weigh the bag in my hand. I hate this shit. Ecstasy is a terrible drug. It's an office worker's high: cheap and artificial. But I cannot let myself fall asleep. I've been asleep for weeks and didn't know it.

No more.

I swallow the pill dry, like the mistake it probably is.

Beside me, the roadway falls silent.

I look out at it:

Maya Kibby thrashes around. Jesse fucks her but she's still got her bra on. Jesse rips it down.

Flat out on the highway, the road like a dark tunnel now. I push the engine as hard as it'll go. *Fucking Sock.* My guess is he's headed back to Gatton, but the truth is he could be going anywhere. The pill comes on and I feel good for no reason. Not super good – the gear is half-garbage – but better than I should. It's a buffer. And below it, as if bobbing underneath the hard ceiling of a frozen lake, are fast visions of the dead girl. I can see Maya now. She's still alive in my mind's eye and I'm shaking the steering wheel, willing those ideas away:

Jesse fucking her from behind, a fistful of her hair.

The road and a line of trees and the road and billboards ('Cherish Life', 'Toyota RAV4', 'A Better Place To Buy') and sale lots of trucks, fresh-fruit barns, solitary pubs, vacant land. There's nothing out here. The townships barely break up the monotony; Helidon comes and goes, Grantham comes and goes, it all comes and goes. It all repeats.

Gatton arrives with the dawn sun. The morning feels unnaturally crisp and serene. I drive into town and across the railway line to Mandy Lowenfield's place in the drive-in theatre. This is a hunch that pays off: Sock's van is outside on the road, the front axle dumped into a drainage ditch and the van's back door open for the world to see.

I get out and look.

Empty. The interior smells of detergent.

Of course it does.

Of course Sock dumped her body for him.

I grab the shotgun.

Jesse laughs, turns to the camera and says, 'Your turn, motherfucker.' The frame locks. The lens warps in and out of focus as Sock steps into sight. He rolls a condom onto his short stubby dick and gently eases himself into Maya. She doesn't say anything. She just watches. Her eyes...

No movement around the house as I come down the drive-in's asphalt plane but I can hear Sock screaming and thrashing around inside the house. There's the sound of collisions, things thrown into walls. I'm beaming from the drug. I'm amped. I creep up on the rear door and Mandy shouts his name: Sock! Her voice sounds muffled and reverberated – *she's in the bathroom*. I circle the house looking for the plumbing downpipes. I find them and peer in through a small window alongside. Mandy stares back at me, her back to the door, a red sports bag at her feet.

'Oh my god, Nate, he's gone fucking crazy. He's tearing the place apart. Go get help.'

'Is he armed?'

'What? No. I don't think so.'

'Stay there.'

'No, Nate, you need to –'

I go back round to the door and take a quick look inside. The kitchen. The bathroom door. A small hallway. Something flies into the kitchen, exploding against the edge of the counter. The wreckage skids to a stop not far from me.

It's a broken printer.

Sock starts screaming again. '... And then where the fuck is... I just know how and where and when... Ah, oh I see...'

Delirious.

'... Ah, ah, oh shit...'

Sock is fucking Maya and Jesse has a hold of her and things start to go bad. She starts to buckle a little then starts to struggle. Nothing seems to set it off. It happens fast. Jesse slides an arm around Maya's throat and whispers something in her ear. Sock, meanwhile, keeps pounding away as if he doesn't notice. Jesse's hollering. Sock's hollering too, 'Ah, ah, ah...'

'... And, it must be, it must be, it must be,' he's saying over and again as I step into the room behind him, the gun locked into my shoulder.

'Sock.'

He's standing in a nest of torn-apart books and kitchen

rubbish. Every bin in the house is in here, turned out on the carpet. He doesn't look good. His skin is the colour of spoilt cream and his eyes are blood-red. He's half-dressed, his belly drooping over black jeans.

'What do you want?' he says, ignoring the gun pointed at him.

'I've come to find you. What are you doing with all this?'

'Uh, I'm...' He shrugs.

'You better sit down,' I say.

'Are you... are you going to shoot me?'

'No. Should I?'

Sock looks at the gun then up at my face. He does this a couple of times: gun, face, gun, face. Finally he rests his gaze on the gun and starts to cry. The tears come slowly at first but soon he's shaking his head, beet-red in the face, wailing like a little kid.

He squats down in the rubbish, arms wrapped around himself. I hear the click of Mandy opening the bathroom door in the other room.

'What are you doing, Sock?' I say.

'Just... looking for... argh, I dunno. I had some... some money, ya know. I was gonna go.'

Jesse's money.

'Where is it?'

'I dunno. I've lost the, the key.'

'What key?'

He doesn't answer.

I look around the room, at the destruction. 'Why did you run back up in Toowoomba?'

'That was you?'

'You left something in the motel.'

His eyes widen. 'What?'

'The tape, you sick fuck.'

'What tape? What tape?'

'You and Maya and Jesse.'

'No, no, no, no, no, no! No! No!' Sock grabs an old tennis shoe from one of the piles and hoists it at me, losing his balance in the process. As he's looking to get back up, I go over and kick him twice in the side. I put my foot on his chest and point the barrel of the shotgun at him. I push down with my foot, feeling his rib cage give a little. Sock groans and scratches at my foot.

'Where's this fucking key?'

'I –'

I kick him again, in the side of the head this time. Like I said, I never liked Sock. Blood trickles out of his mouth. My stomach tightens but the drug is floating around inside me, turning everything into a movie.

'What are you looking for?'

'This,' says Mandy. She's standing there behind us, the red sports bag in her hand.

'Okay,' I say. 'Now what happened to Jesse?'

'What?' says Sock.

'He's dead. What happened to him?'

Sock looks over at Mandy and the sports bag.

'Hey! Talk to me. Did you kill him?'

'*Me?* I thought Iris… No man, christ. I don't know what… He fucking deserved it. He fucking did, man, but I didn't do it. Oh man, fuck. Oh man, I didn't want this, I didn't want any of it. Oh god. He fucking made me. I didn't want to film that day, I didn't want any of it.'

Jesse is smiling and Maya Kibby is struggling and he doesn't let her go until she stops moving. Sock's wailing, 'What are you doing? What are you doing?' He pushes Jesse away from the body but it's too late. Jesse rubs his hands and twitches and says, 'Piss off, I barely touched her.'

'I know he killed her, Sock. I saw it. You left a fucking videotape of it in your room back up on the mountain.'

'What?' says Mandy.

'No, no, no, no –'

I kick him again. 'Enough of that shit. I should fucking shoot you.'

'I could tell, I shoulda... He was angry before we even started and I just shoulda...'

'Should have what, Sock? Come on, tell me.'

'I should have stopped him.'

'You think?'

Sock looks up at me.

'Was he like that?' I say.

'Sometimes.'

'I never saw him like that.'

'You didn't know him like we knew him. He was...' and he starts to blubber again. 'Iris, man. She knew what he was. Only me and Iris.'

'What?'

'He went crazy, just fucking crazy, man. But I didn't think he'd...'

'What the fuck?' says Mandy. 'Who are you talking about? What is he saying? Nate, what's he saying?'

I stomp down hard on Sock's groin and he splutters. It stops him moving long enough for me to walk over to Mandy and grab the bag out of her hands. I rip it open.

Another bag of pills.

And a set of keys on a yellow XXXX Bitter lanyard.

Mandy puts her hand back out for the bag and I push her off. She stumbles back into the kitchen and trips over the printer from before. 'You... you can't just take that,' she yells.

I point at the refrigerator. The Missing Person flyer of

Maya still taped up to the door. Maya's still smiling in her felt-pen sunglasses, saying *I'm Dead! Boo! Hoo!*

'Her.'

Mandy looks. Then looks back, confused.

'Her. That's who he's talking about.'

'What?'

I turn back to Sock. He's trying to sit up. He's trying to watch us. A dumbfounded look on his face.

'I gotta… I gotta. I gotta go,' says Mandy, breathing through her mouth, finally getting it.

'Yeah, that might be a good idea.'

When she's gone, I beat Sock senseless, his warm blood stinging my hands and face. It's brutal. Some cold, blank impulse seems to get me through it. I don't want to kill him but once I start hitting him – properly hitting him – it's difficult to stop. His pain feels good to me. The blood, the slap of his bones and flesh against my fist. I want more of it.

'What are you doing? What are you doing?'

This piece of shit.

I'd prefer to be hitting Jesse but blood is blood at this point.

The only thing is: Sock saves himself. He gives it up. He starts talking, yelling actually.

'The money's buried! It's – ugh – buried!'

It's in a box down by the old drive-in screen.

I find a shovel and we go down there. Sock staggers along. I follow with the gun trained on him. Summer radiates off the bitumen. We reach the bottom of the tarmac where the decrepit screen towers over us. Sock grunts and veers off to the right, leading me into a small grove of trees on the drive-in's outer edge. We're not far into the knee-high grass there, just out of sight, when he slumps himself down beside a small cleared area. The soil there is freshly disturbed.

'Sock, if you move, I'll bury you here.'

I start digging.

It takes a while and the scrub we're in is like a furnace. I'm wet with sweat when the shovel grinds into something hard. I dig it out. It's a green locker, like something from an army disposal store.

There's a padlock.

The key from the red gym back slips right in and I snap the lock open and lift the lid:

Another bag. A big black duffle.

I open it.

Jesse's money. Packed in plastic wrap. It's a fortune, maybe more than I've estimated. I can barely lift the bag out of the locker.

The relief is so enormous that I desperately need to piss. I urinate into the empty locker. Sock stares at me as I do this so I turn and water up and down the leg of his jeans. It's petty and cruel and Sock just keeps on looking at me, somehow more hurt and scared by it than any of the violence from before. When it's done, I zip up and walk out of the brush and leave him there.

I drive with a full car of things:

Two bags of pills.

A duffle bag full of cash.

Half an ounce of weed.

A suitcase full of amateur pornography.

A ledger.

A sawn-off shotgun.

A tape of my childhood friend having sex.

A tape of my other friend killing a woman.

It's morning now. Bright out. Gatton doesn't look so good any more.

You deserve it. You deserve it. You deserve…

It's true: all the good and the bad.

I called this in.

This is what I turn over in my mind as I drive the car into the forest country by Pinchy's house – I pass Casa del Gangbang, in fact – and then further out into the back roads, without any idea where I'm headed. I drive until I spot a half-dozen blackened forty-gallon drums dumped by the side of the road. The area is thick with tall trees and shrubs and there's grass growing down the centre of the road. I stop and count out forty-five grand for Dennis and Hatch then I take the rest of the money and drag it into the wilderness and re-bury it. When I'm done with that I take the suitcase of porn – and the tape of Jesse killing Maya, and the tape of Iris – and I dump all of it into one of the drums by the road and set it on fire.

I burn everything that ties the money to all this sinister garbage.

Pitch-black smoke rises up.

It's 10:20 a.m.

It's a Monday.

I think I'm having some kind of episode because I don't want to go home. I have an 11:30 Macroeconomics lecture in Morrison Hall. I could make it after a shower.

There's a sense of relief. It takes a moment to notice why.

I won, I guess.

'And you've all seen this before, I'm sure. We have real GDP along the X-axis and, running up the Y is price. What about this plotted here? What is this line? Anyone? Anyone? Aggregate Demand. This is the Big Daddy, the demand for all the goods and services in a country and, and, *and...*' The lecturer snaps his fingers, trying to get a response from the auditorium.

I block it out.

I close my eyes.

The other students murmur around me. Pens scratch at paper. Sips are taken from coffee cups. Arses move in chairs.

I pretend I'm asleep.

'Nate?'

Someone touches my shoulder. My eyes open. The auditorium is empty except for a couple of students walking down the far side of the hall. Samantha Kline is standing over me. It feels like a year since I slept in her dorm room.

'Nate?' she says again.

'Yeah. I think I fell asleep.'

I start getting my stuff together. Sam sits down beside me. She looks worried.

'Do I look that bad?'

'I heard about Jesse,' she says. 'I'm so sorry.'

I don't know what to say. I stare ahead. I think I'm nodding, slowly.

'Is there going to be a service or something?' she says.

'I don't know.'

'What happened?'

'I don't know.'

'Come here,' and Sam slips an arm around me and lays her head on my shoulder. She smells of cloves and cigarette smoke. She puts a hand over my hand and tells me I need to lie down for a bit.

An announcement is posted in the residential halls: *Gatton University student Jesse Koerstz was involved in a violent incident on the night of Wednesday the 14th of September or Thursday the 15th. The police are looking for people to come forward, specifically anyone who may have seen Koerstz or know of his whereabouts for the days in question.*

'It's a big deal,' says Sam as I stare at the photocopied poster with Jesse's stupid face on it. 'The vice chancellor made the morning news. He told everyone that Gatton was completely safe, but it doesn't feel safe, does it?'

Back in her room – afterwards – Sam puts a T-shirt on and tells me that people have been hooking up all over campus. 'Alison totally got back with her ex. My ex tried to booty-call me last night. It's death, right? It makes people horny. It's so weird. People are gonna be down for it tonight.'

'Is there something on?'

'The campus club is hosting a memorial piss-up for him.'

'For Jesse?'

She nods.

Jesse hated the club. He never went there.

Good.

'You going?'

Sam sighs. 'I don't know.'

'You have class this arvo?'

'Trying to get rid of me?'

'I gotta crash. I can't go back to mine. Every dickhead in Gatton is going to be dropping by to score or offer their condolences or something.'

'What about your friend? Is she okay?'

'Iris?'

'Yeah.'

'No one knows what Iris is doing.'

It's late afternoon when I come to. I have a feeling Sam has been and gone but I can't be sure. There's a fresh towel on the end of the bed. I go downstairs and take a shower. The Thynne Hall bathroom is pretty much the same as my old one in Riddell. I stand in the hot spray and bright lights and after a few minutes, my hands start to shake. My vision crowds. The walls contract.

I start to cough.

The coughing keeps going. I vomit a few times until it's pure bile. I'm sobbing, my hands scratch at my chest and face and scalp but I don't feel it. It's like it's happening to someone else. This goes on for a long time, twenty minutes or so, until a guy walks into the cubicle beside me and asks me if I'm okay, and the act of having to speak, to say, 'No, I'm fine', seems to bring me back together.

A dark grey dusk and my car sits in the car park with all the others. There's no one around. I'm alone. I open the trunk and check on all the terrible things in there.

Nothing's changed:

Gun.

Money.

Drugs.

My beeper.

I check it. It's full of call-back messages. I ignore them.

There's a public phone by the mouth of the car park. I pop a coin in and press the digits for Iris. She doesn't pick up.

I think about the finish line.

Pay off Dennis and Hatch.

Wait until this blows over, then bank the rest of Jesse's money.

I need to tell Iris this. She might show at the campus club.

I stare at the phone.

Dad. I should call Dad. Pick up this phone and call him and tell him that I love him, in case something happens.

I punch the number.

It rings. There's a piercing click and a recording of my mother's voice:

You've reached the Byrne residence. We're not in at the moment so if you'd like to leave your name and –

I slam the receiver down.

My mother's voice sets me off.

This is not how my life is supposed to go.

Fucking Jesse.

The column of smoke rising up out of smouldering videotapes.

Maya's eyes.

I want to talk to Iris. I go back to the car and grab the weed and neck another pill, then another. I figure I own this batch now and right now it feels like the only way back to straight and clear.

The campus club is so crowded that security have the front doors open and the party is spilling out onto the lawn. It's 7:35 p.m. but people are 11:30-drunk. They're shouting at each other, sucking face, falling over. As I push through the throng, I don't hear a word about Jesse and the murder. Almost none of these people are our friends. Everyone's here to see everyone else.

Inside, there's a crowd of people standing around the tiny dance floor. A slide show runs against a white wall behind it. I watch the images flicker by:

Jesse doing group work.

Jesse clowning around in the halls.

Jesse in the library.

There are photos of him at the pub, in people's houses, sitting on the hood of a car. I watch a picture of myself appear and disappear. There's a photo of Iris and Sock and Jesse standing by a horse. There's a house party, a keg party, a crowd shot from a gig.

Jesse dressed up for winter.

Jesse holding someone's cat.

The music blaring over the PA has no bearing on any of this. 'Confide In Me' by Kylie Minogue. Jesse was a rock guy. He told me he didn't like the sound of women singing.

Jesse at the beach.

Jesse in sunglasses.

Jesse in a mirror.

Jesse and Maya Kibby.

Jesse and Maya Kibby, again.

No one's watching. No one sees it, displayed wall-sized in front of them.

None of us saw it.

Except Sock.

And Iris. That's what he said, wasn't it:

'Iris, man. She knew what he was. Me and Iris.'

I press my eyes shut and bury my face in my hands. *Is this how bad people make their way through the world?* I assumed they looked like Dennis and Hatch, like outlaws.

But do bad people look like good people, like friends and brothers and boyfriends and students, until they have their hands around your throat? I stand there and a part of me thinks the answer is yes. All of these men standing around me, drinks in hand, backs to the screen – to Jesse and Maya – these men are smiling, laughing, flirting, and they look harmless. Completely harmless. But any one of them could be something else now: a rapist, a murderer, a spree-shooter, a torturer, a paedophile. I try to picture them sprayed with blood and gore and it's easy. It's *so* easy. All of these guys could be Jesse because all of these guys were just like him, right up until he –

The photos continue:

Jesse in the library.

Jesse's face close-up, pupils blazed.

Jesse and Iris.

I feel another crying jag coming on. It could be the pills kicking in. I can feel everyone's naivety and stupidity and pain. It's like a current flowing through the air.

I push back through the crowd. A girl from Intro to Accounting last year gives me a hug and hands me a plastic cup full of beer. A guy I sell weed to tells me he's sorry. A half-dozen people try to talk to me but I brush them off. I ask everyone if they've seen Iris and some of them have and some of them haven't, but no one says she's here tonight. On the far side of the club, as far away from the slide show as possible, there's a guy standing alone, propped up with his back against the wall, ashing a cigarette into a planter box. It's Craig, Jesse's other dealer. He raises his head when he sees me. Almost smiles.

'Quite the turnout,' he says. 'It's a fucking bummer about Jesse.'

I look at him hard. *Could Craig have killed Jesse?* It comes out of nowhere because, as tired and mashed as I am, I realise I don't really know what happened to Jesse. I don't really care who killed him.

'Yeah,' I say.

'How you holding up?'

'I'm okay.'

'You hear about Sock?'

'What?'

'People are saying he did it. That he killed him.'

I shrug. 'Maybe.'

'Maybe?'

'I haven't seen him.'

'That's not what I'm hearing, man.'

'Really?'

'It's just not what I'm hearing.'

'*Really?*'

He purses his lips, eyes dead ahead.

'Well then, what do you hear, Craig?'

'That you're all spooked and shit. That you've been running him down, sleeping in your car and stuff.' He glances at me. 'Did Sock do that?'

'What?'

'Your face?'

'No.'

'Well, Iris is fucking freaking out, man. She's worried. She's talking a blue streak about leaving town. Has been for days now. She sounds like shit,' he says, changing gears and delivering this as if it were small talk. 'And I can't find her.'

'When did you last see her?'

'Who?'

'Fuck, Craig, *Iris*. When did you see Iris?'

'I haven't seen her. She just called the house.'

'And?'

'And that's none of your business.'

'Craig.'

'Nate.'

'When was this? The call.'

'Oh, sometime on the weekend, I guess. She called a few times, got the machine. It's hard to hit her back.' Craig runs a hand through his hair, neatening it for no reason. I can see now that some of this is for show. Something is concealed. There's a very thin line of sweat along his brow. 'You spoken to the cops?' he says.

'Me? No. Have you?'

Craig looks around. 'Yeah, the local guys are idiots. They came to my place. They asked me some questions about Jesse, just bullshit stuff like, *Had I seen him on this day and this day* and whatever. I think they're looking for Sock, mainly. They've been hitting every share house he's ever been to apparently. I've spent half the day calling round telling people to hide their shit.'

'Did they mention Iris?'

'Yeah, they're looking for her too.'

More to myself than him, I say, 'You reckon she's coming tonight?'

He laughs. 'Fat chance. Look at these arseholes.'

Craig's right. *What am I doing?*

We stop talking and people-watch. After a time, Craig lights another cigarette and says, 'It's funny, isn't it?' It creeps me out. The pills are taking a dark turn. The whole thing is sliding on me. I walk into the crowd and I'm only a few people deep when I hear Craig yelling after me. The music pumps and everyone's voices are like sirens. I have no idea what Craig's saying. He could be telling me the answers or cussing me out and I don't care. I catch one last look at him but he's just standing there, motionless, as if he never said anything.

I can't be sure what's happening.

The night air has heat in it. I'm jogging. My feet fall heavily, in and out of time with the thump of the club behind me. I'm in the back streets of campus. Then I'm running the Ring Road, the pasture fields in front of me. Then, I'm lost. I go down to a barbed-wire fence and stare out at an empty paddock. The black silhouettes of trees in the grass.

I eventually find my car.

I don't know what time it is.

I don't know how long I've been walking.

My blood still feels bright in my veins and the streetlights have the warm hue of a Christmas decoration. There's a breeze on my chest and shoulders. I don't know what I've done with my shirt. I look down at my hands and there it is:

I'm holding it.

I'm holding my shirt.

I lay the shirt out on the hood of the car. It feels wet so I run my hands over the fabric, smoothing out wrinkles. As I'm doing this, I hear footfall and look up. A man stands two cars over. He's wearing a cowboy hat.

'Nate?' he says, his voice like gravel.

'I think my shirt's wet,' I say.

The man nods and hands grab at me, dragging me back and punching me. The back of my head collects cold metal.

Clunk.

The world goes from night to black.

The car moves along the highway and no one speaks. There's four of them. The driver has long dark-coloured hair pinned back with a bandana. In the passenger seat sits the man in the cowboy hat from the car park. He's still in the hat; the peak of it brushes the car's interior. Beside me in the back are two men, crowding me in. I'm too scared to look at either of them but they both have beards. They both stink of leather and grime. The whole car feels dank with sweat.

They're bikies.

I cough, clear my throat. 'Am I in trouble?'

The man on my right huffs.

The cowboy says, 'That depends.'

A motorcycle overtakes us. The rider wears a denim vest patched at the back. The bike's indicator light comes on.

I recognise the car interior then. This is my car.

'Depends on what?' I say.

'You'll see,' says the cowboy.

We turn into a dirt road. The rider from before stands beside an open gate and waves us through. There's a sign there and it reads:

WELCOME TO HELL.

I start puking the moment they let me out. We're parked in a clearing beside a squat brick building, some kind of bunker in the wilderness. The ground is warm under my hands. When I'm done, the two guys from before pick me up and drag me along by the armpits.

It's not much brighter inside the bunker. The building is a big airless space, half-full of people, mostly men. Music plays. Hard rock I don't recognise. I crane my head, looking for any sign of hope. There's a small vacant stage, a shitty bar (like something out of a suburban rumpus room), two pool tables and a collection of mismatched furniture. Down the far end, a group of men stand in a wide circle. They dump me in the middle of that circle.

'This is him,' says the one in the cowboy hat. 'I think he's a bit fucked up. So stay clear. He's been throwing up.'

The floor is dry exposed concrete. Someone comes and stands in front of my hands. Two huge boots covered in blunt steel studs, the tips worn down from wear. I don't look up at the rest.

'You Nate?' says the voice above. There's a slight drawl to it.

I nod.

'You can look at me. I'm not the bloody Queen, mate,' he says.

Murmurs of laughter.

I look. The man is short and wide, a bearded gnome face peering down at me over a beer gut. He'd be comical if it weren't for the eyes: two small black dots in his face, turning the rest of it sinister. Under these eyes, there are dull tattoos smudged into his cheeks.

'Been looking all over for you, kid.'

I nod.

'Yeah, I'm real interested to have a chat with you,' he says. 'I hear you sell a bit of weed?'

I glance around at the other men. They're all shadowy iterations of this man in front of me. More beards, hair, tattoos. I don't recognise any them. The circle is tight. I'm within kicking distance of everyone.

'It's okay, mate,' says the man in front. 'I'll wager that it's our stuff you're selling.'

'Where am I?'

I get kicked. The air blasts out of me like a burst paper bag. I heave and choke.

'Hey! Nah, let him ask questions. He's okay. Jesus, Roachy, you're fucking raring, aren't you?'

More laughter, louder this time.

'Pick him up. I'll do my back in talking to this cunt like this. Put him on something, Robbo.'

They drag over a bar stool. I'm hoisted onto it and held in place.

'Now, kid... what's his name again? What was it? Nate. Okay. Now, Nate, see this?' The man points to a small woven badge on his vest where his heart is. A posse of skeletons ride motorcycles inside a woven circle. The words *Doomed Forever* and *Forever Doomed* wrap around the edges. 'You heard of the Doomriders? This is our clubhouse. I'm the bloke in charge. You can call me Murph. And you know what? Not many people get to come out here, Nate. You're a pretty special guy tonight. And the reason you're here is that we have ourselves a bit of a problem that we think you can help us out with. We do, don't we, boys?'

No one answers. No one says a word. The music keeps playing but everyone stands there silently. They're all waiting for something.

'The problem we have, and I hope you can help us with this Nate, I really do, for your sake. The problem we have is that we've got these blokes in our midst who are trying to dog the bloody lot of us. And jeez, Nate, it makes me angry, so fucking angry. Even just

181

talkin' about it fires me up. Christ. Here, give me that.'

A hand reaches out and gives Murph a can of beer. He chugs it down, wipes the foam from his beard. 'Now, as I was saying. I got these blokes who are trying to fuck us. You met any new blokes lately, blokes like us?'

I nod.

'What were they calling themselves?' says Murph.

My mind is completely blank. 'I... I...'

A hand clips the back of my head. Another set of hands steadies me on the chair.

'Give him a sec,' says Murph.

'Dennis,' I say, at last. 'I can't remember the other one. He was smaller.'

They all laugh at that.

'Ooooo, Hatch wouldn't like that, no, not at all,' says Murph. 'But then again, fuck him. Now, you see, those are the blokes I'm talking about. I hear they've been giving you a bit of a hard time? If I were a betting man, and christ knows I am, I'd bet they were the ones who tuned up your face like that.'

I nod.

'And I figure they want their money? Is that it? Yeah?'

I nod again.

'This is where it gets a bit bloody tricky. You know what that money is about?'

'Pills, I think.'

'That's right!' he says. 'Holy shit. Do you know where those pills come from?'

'You?'

'Close. Have another bloody guess?'

I can't think of an answer. 'I don't know.'

Murph grabs me by the hair at the back of my head and brings those death eyes in close to me. 'The fucking pigs,' he says. 'Taken from a house of ours down in Brisbane two months ago, and now here they are, in sunny fucking Gatton. My own fucking guys flipping them to fucking students. It's enough to make me sick. If I didn't do a stint with... ' Murph looks away. He lets me go. 'Damn. Sorry, kid. I get bloody wound up talking about this stuff. You don't... it's not bloody you, is it? What I want you to tell me is whether or not your dead mate bought the gear from those two idiots?'

'I... I don't know. I think so.'

'Who else was moving it?'

'I don't know.'

He drops a heavy elbow into my thigh.

'Argh, argh... Sock,' I say. 'This other guy.'

'Sock? Oh yeah, I think I've heard about this kid. We're looking for him, right?' he says to someone. 'What about the cunt? Doris? Delores.'

I start to shake my head.

A voice behind me says, 'Iris.'

'No, no, not her. She doesn't have anything to do with this.'

Murph slaps me. Then he slaps me again.

'That's what she reckons but I dunno, kid. I just don't know what to do with you. Hold on.' He turns to confer with the others. 'Okay, okay,' he says. 'Shit. Okay. You're right. Shit. I must be tired. I *am* bloody tired, tired of you lot. Okay, Nate, one more thing. How'd you go, running that shit down for Dennis? I don't suppose you found any of it, right? And tell me, because we're about to take you outside and shoot you.'

I'm zoning in and out now. Still, when I hear this, my body pushes out a short chuckle.

'Is he?' says someone.

I'm panting, trying to talk. The music feels loud again. The room, it's a dream. It's all a bad dream.

Murph comes in real close. His breath entering my mouth.

'Kid?' he says.

'It's in the car. It's all in the boot of the car.'

They can't remember who has the keys to my car and minutes pass as the bikies pat down their pockets and argue with one another. Murph's furious. *Didn't any of you dickheads check the fucking car?* Eventually the keys are found and they drag me outside, making me unlock the boot. It pops. One of the bikies has a flashlight and he shines it in there. He curses under his breath as the beam passes over everything.

'Well?' shouts Murph, standing in the bunker's doorway.

'He's not lying,' says one of them.

'Boss, he's got all sorts of shit in here,' says another. 'All sorts of gear.' And he holds up my shotgun.

'Whoa. I'm impressed, kid,' says Murph.

I say, 'What now?'

They take me out back anyway.

We go in through the clubhouse and across to another door, and then back outside and across the clearing and into a forest of scrub so dark I trip and fall within the first thirty seconds. The whole club follows us, a wandering tribe in the night. I can hear them as the path snakes through the trees and pours us out into a wide-open prairie field further on. A half-moon sits overhead. We walk out into the field for a minute until we come to an old caravan surrounded by knee-high grass. A man stands guard beside it.

'Any trouble?' says the cowboy.

'No, they've been quiet,' says the man on guard.

'Okay, let's get this over with,' says Murph.

Two of the bigger men open the caravan door and go in. There's muted thumping inside. The walls of the van shake. Three hooded bodies are dragged out, all of them squirming. The three of them are dropped to the ground. Murph shines a light down: they're all handcuffed.

'Hey there,' says Murph. He waves a hand.

The cowboy removes the hoods, one at a time:

Dennis.

Hatch.

Iris.

'No, no, no…' It's my voice.

Hands hold me back.

Dennis looks barely conscious. Hatch squints around, his eyes swollen shut. Iris is less banged up but she has dirt and blood on her face.

Hatch says, 'Murph, Murph, we can –'

He's punched.

'We can't,' says Murph. 'Aunt Cindy ain't going to like that this is how you ended up, Hatch, but… this is where you ended up.'

Hatch spots me then.

'Yeah, I bought a friend to see you,' says Murph.

'It's… it's… *He's* the one who –'

Another blow.

'Yeah, okay,' says Murph. 'Put them over there. Put the kid down next to them.'

I go cold.

'No, wait,' I say.

They take Hatch and Dennis's cuffs off and push them to the ground. I get punched in the stomach – that puts me down. They then pull me over and put me beside the other two bikers. For some reason they stand Iris up, away from us, and she's looking at me now. She's in shock, swaying a little, eyes white and open.

'Wait, wait,' I say.

'What?' says Murph. He has a gun in his hands. He's checking it.

'I gave you the money. I got your stuff back.'

'I know you did, kid. But the problem is, I can't have you running around, knowing what you know.'

'I don't know anything.'

'All these people out here could get into strife if I don't put you down with these two. You're just... What do they call it?'

'Collateral,' says the one in the cowboy hat.

'Collateral,' says Murph.

'But... What the...'

They turn me round.

An open field at night. No breeze. No trees.

Hatch blubbering beside me.

Dark grass.

Silence.

Iris.

Then, the slotting of a rifle.

I try to stare at the moon. My vision blurs and refocuses: vapour trails of white in the sky. I'm going to die in front of Iris and I can't even see straight. That makes a measure of sense. But there's something else. It's in the distance, out over the fences and fields and halfway to the horizon. I can hear the droning rattle of a train coming along the tracks.

They say our brains remember everything. That our subconscious is like a surveillance camera, tracking every move, recording every misstep. Every detail. Everything, from birth to death: my brother, my mother, my high school, my undergraduate degree, one phase leading to the next. Part of me has it all logged.

Day to day, I know I can't forget these things so I work on the connections instead. I work on the sequence. I chop that apart. These are the things I try to stamp the light out of with booze and weed. No sequence, no connection and thus no repetition and no pattern. When I'm out of it, swaying on my feet at home in my caravan, there's a blankness that settles in. I'm a clean slate then because there's nothing left to bind my life together. Even in death, even in this field just outside Gatton, I'm fucked up on drugs, just a wall without mortar.

A few months earlier, something happened. In any other person's mind, it would have been a warning, but not mine. I don't have a good sense of these things, like I said. I don't see the signs. And so it just came and went...

There was a party at Johnny Mouth's.

Early August. A Tuesday night.

Jesse and I hadn't seen much of each other. He was deep

into his thing with Iris. And business was booming. I wrote his absence off as a busy friend.

I know better now.

Now, the dates line up like bad weather. Jesse was busy paving his way to this mess. Videotaping women. Getting into pills. Making deals with rogue bikies. Giving himself over to terrifying impulses.

The party at Johnny Mouth's is like a mirage now, sitting in the middle of all that. Another bad memory pushed to the bottom. Another weird episode in amongst the rest of everything that happened, forgotten in the rush. The rush to this field and these men and death.

The low drone of the train echoes across the plains and drowns out the beginning:

'– Wait, wait, Jesus –'

A voice from the crowd.

Hatch says something and makes a scrambled run for it. Everyone's so distracted, he actually gets up and runs down into the field.

'Murph, I can – Oh my god, oh my,' and she's so panicked she can't speak properly. 'Murph,' she says, and the tone says it all.

I recognise the voice.

Iris.

Iris has come back to life.

True to form, Johnny Mouth would not shut his fucking face. 'And oh my god, there is nothing more messed up than Die Hard II. *It's like the exact point where Hollywood started dropping off. It's like the whole point of* Die Hard II *is to mess up* Die Hard I. *To say, Hey there, dude, so you enjoyed this movie but now we're going to take this thing you liked so much and just smear dogshit on it. That's what that movie says. Damn, man, it's like seeing a statue pulled over.'*

Willy Clinton is taking all this in. He's nodding.

I'm staring across at the two of them. In fact, I'm more staring at Willy's Alice In Chains tee. He has a strip of black gaffer tape pasted to the shirt's interior, down near the waistline, and I can see the light side of the tape through the holes in the front of his shirt there. He's got the tape plastered there so he can twist open his beers without creating more holes in his favourite shirt. But now there's part of a corn chip stuck down there. Or what looks like a corn chip. I'm staring at this because I'm super stoned.

'I kinda liked it,' says Willy.

Johnny actually sputters. 'Wha–, what? You can't, you can't just kinda like it, man. That's like kinda liking,' and he does air quotes, 'the Third Reich or cancer or, I don't know. I mean –'

'Fuck you,' says Willy. 'Fuck you, I can like whatever the hell I like. And let me tell you –'

The piece of corn chip falls off Willy's shirt. I follow it to the floor. There's glitter ground into Johnny's carpet. Good, I think to myself. Glitter is impossible to get out of carpet. There's also at least half a dozen bottle caps down there as well. I'm still transfixed by the garbage on the floor when the party changes gear across the room. There's louder voices. Hands are slapped in high-fives.

I look up.

Jesse.

He takes his time moving through, but he circles round, nods at Johnny and Willy, puts his arm around my shoulder. 'Come with me,' he says, steering me out onto the verandah.

It's dark out. Another quiet night in Gatton except for the rattle of Johnny's air-conditioner on the wall nearby.

'Long time, no see,' Jesse says.

'I guess. Figured you were busy.'

'Always,' he says.

'How's Iris?'

'Ah, good, man. She's crazy but she's good. She's out back. You wanna go find her? Actually, we'll go find her after I smoke this.'

Jesse lights one of his immaculately rolled joints. He has a little rolling machine he uses; he likes to prep these things before coming out.

'So what have you been up to?' he says. 'That money keeps coming in. Who knew those horti fucks would love our green so much? I always figured they'd grow their own?'

'Yeah. Totally.'

'Who else do you have? I can't keep up.'

'Got a lot of Shelton Hall stitched up. There's a kid in there who's buying in bulk and cutting it up but he's not moving it anywhere else so I'm letting him do it.'

'Sounds good to me. What else? You getting your dick wet? You know, I saw that Chloe girl the other day. Looked straight through me.'

I smile at that. 'She wasn't a big fan.'

'Really?'

'Yeah, Chloe was like that.'

'Did she know about…'

'She knew what I did. And she was smart enough to know I wasn't exactly the brains of the operation.'

'Not sure I am either,' he says. 'Strictly speaking. There's something coming up you might be interested in.' Jesse looks around before pulling a small plastic bag from his pocket, three purple tablets inside. 'Now, I know you don't usually do this shit but… Iris found me a chemist, a kid doing an ag-science degree and he looked up how to test this stuff. It's easy as hell apparently. He just mixes something with it, then watches what happens.'

'And Iris found him?'

'Yeah. Some people are still scared of it. There's heaps of people like you. So she's like, if we can kinda guarantee this stuff, imagine how much more we could move. If it's safe, it'll sell itself.'

'And what's this then?' I nod at the bag in his hand.

'First guaranteed batch. Pure as the driven snow, man. My guy says so. And, you know, just for, like, an extra guarantee, I took one of these an hour ago and I'm fine.' He moves his smoke to the other hand and carefully taps a pill out of the bag. 'So it's now or never, Nate. You want to try it, this is as safe as it gets.'

Jesse holds it out to me.

After everything with my brother and all my hang-ups and reservations, this could have been a big moment, a rush of memory and anxiety, a distillation, a test.

It isn't.

I feel like I've been missing out, so I take the drug from him and put it in my mouth, washing it down with a gulp of beer.

I'm knocked to the ground in the field and heavy footfall surrounds me. I roll onto my side and watch a group of men run after Hatch. There's a lot of them, a lot of shouting. There's the train in the distance. And there's an argument behind me. I look up and see Dennis – this giant of a man – and he's standing there alongside me, staring out at the train.

We're in Iris's car. Jesse's driving. Craig's in the passenger seat. A girl I don't know is on one side, Iris is on the other.

'It's good, isn't it?' says Jesse.

Everyone murmurs agreement.

It's better than good.

We come down the hill of Woodlands Road and turn into Yates Street then drive down Goltz until we're in Jesse's driveway. We go into the house and it's dark and stuffy with the day's heat. He turns the TV on before the lights. Music blares out. Images flicker. Video clips:

Something heavy.

Something acoustic.

Something pop.

By the time I pull my gaze from the screen, Craig and the girl are making out, her skirt hiked up over her arse as she sits in his lap. I go to the kitchen where Iris is heating popcorn in the microwave. Jesse's there. They're both sipping on tins of beer, neither saying much.

Jesse leers at me under the kitchen lights.

There's a cracking sound.

I watch the bag turn in the microwave, the tiny yellow world inside.

'Here,' he says. Something cold and hard thuds against my chest and drops to the floor.

He laughs.

I squat down and look: an open tin of VB. I put my hand into the pool of white foam spilling out of the can and run my fingers through. It's beautiful. The bubbles in the beer crackle softly. I scoop up the tin and take a drink.

'It's a good drug,' I say.

'We're going to be rich,' says Jesse.

'Uh-huh,' says Iris.

She opens the bag of popcorn and lets the steam out. Leaving it to cool on the counter, she comes over and drapes her arms around my neck, pulling me into the centre of the kitchen. We dance a slow dance with Jesse stamping out a dull beat with the heel of his palm.

'Nate, Nate, Nate,' she whispers.

We keep dancing.

'I never knew you guys grew up together,' says Jesse. 'I thought it might have been a high-school thing. How long has it been?'

'Forever,' says Iris. 'For ever and ever.'

'That's a long time,' says Jesse.

He slips down from the counter and comes over, puts his arms around both of us. It feels wonderful. It feels right. The three of us sway in time to some new silent song, our heads touching, hair and scalp grinding.

'Let's go inside,' says Iris.

Iris screams, 'He can... Nate can help you! He knows how to do things! He can work for you, he can –'

'Shut the fuck up,' says Murph. He turns towards me, then he looks out past me and says, 'What are they doing out there?' Out in the field, the men are working over Hatch, standing out in the night beating him to death. Murph slaps another bikie on the arm. 'Tell them to cut that out.'

More men run out. A small fight breaks out but they soon stop. Hatch slumps to the ground and the rest of them stand and wait, looking back at us.

Iris says, 'I'm begging you, he can help, he can do things, he can work for you, you have to –' Her voice squeaks as she's punched. She lands on the ground not far from me. 'Please,' she gasps. 'We'll... we'll work it off. He's studying business. He can do paperwork, sell for you, he can... we'll do anything... we'll...'

'She's right, Murph,' says a voice.

I look over. It's Dennis.

'Shit,' says Murph.

There's a murmuring in the crowd.

'The girl's right,' says Dennis a second time.

Everyone stops. Everyone waits.

Dennis looks at them. 'Well, are you fucks gonna do this or not?'

'What'd you say?' Murph takes something off another man and moves towards Dennis. 'What did you say, fucker?'

'You heard me.'

'Oh, well, excuse me, Dennis,' says Murph and as he says it, I see that the thing in his hand is a gun. He lifts it up to Dennis's head and the shot cracks and echoes. Black blood sprays out of his head. And yet Dennis still raises a hand to the hole in his skull as he slumps down to the ground, like some part of his life is momentarily still in there.

Out in the field, Hatch screams.

We go to Jesse's bedroom and Iris kisses me. Her lips are on my lips. She doesn't hurry. She's doesn't push on me. There's a weird tenderness to it, like we're trying to make this big mistake as slowly as possible. I run a hand through her hair and it feels like I always thought it would, like warm ribbon, like tiny threads.

Her body is pulled back but her lips stay on me. She kisses my neck, a hand holding the back of my head. I open my eyes and Jesse is standing there behind her, trying to get her denim skirt loose.

He looks at me and winks and I see it in monstrous slow motion:

That eye.

The lid winding down over a glassy red pupil and rolling back up.

The black centre.

It's all in there. Always was if I ever cared to look.

The warning.

***

Murph turns to me.

'Is this true? Can you do accounts?' he says, like he hasn't just killed a man right in front of me.

I'm dragged up. 'Yeah, yes.'

'Because I just fired the last guy,' he says, taking a moment to spit on Dennis's body. 'Okay, then. Give him that gun of his.'

Someone thrusts my sawn-off shotgun into my hands. My first instinct is to kill Murph, to sweep the thing up and blow his head clean off.

'Careful,' says Murph. 'Shit, kid. Okay, first bit of bookkeeping is your old mate Hatch. Go and shoot him.'

'What?'

'You heard me.'

'No... no... I...'

'Yes,' says Murph.

They turn me round and push me towards where Hatch is lying. He's about thirty metres out into the field.

'Go on,' says Murph.

I find I'm not so steady on my feet. Every part of my body is as heavy as concrete. I shuffle out, the gun pulling down on my arm. The men surrounding Hatch break off and walk back in. We pass each other; they part around me. As I come up on Hatch, I see him as not much more than a dark shape on the ground. But I can just make out his face, bloodied and open and white. He's on his back, an arm holding onto his side and the other trying to push himself away from me.

'No,' he says and he gasps, just getting the word out. 'No.'

That's all he has.

I turn back to the crowd. 'I can't.'

Murph grabs Iris by the hair and puts his gun to her head. 'You want her to die, kid? *You want to die?*'

Iris is crying. She says something but I can't hear it, not out here.

I check the gun. I replay that day of shooting practice in the forest, the bark ripping from the trees, the retort of the gun against my shoulder.

Hatch starts huffing in and out.

One last look at him:

A thin weaselly man in a field.

The gentle buzz of insects. The sway of the grass.

The faint clacking of the train on the tracks, now long passed but still reaching me from a distance.

'Come on,' yells Murph.

Hatch's breath:

In.

Out.

My own breath:

In.

'I'm sorry,' I say.

'Jesus! Jesus fucking christ,' screams Murph. I hear him running and he's on me faster than seems possible, the two of us suddenly down in the grass with his fist slamming into the side of my head. When he's done, the world is black around the edges.

'Give me that fucking gun. Now, say goodnight, nephew.'

Fire bursts in the darkness. The shot is close and deafening.

Hatch makes a terrible squelching sound. By some miracle of biology he's still alive, still begging through it, still getting a soft wail out through the gurgling.

Murph fires again.

There's nothing after that.

FOREVER

In October, I start work for the Doomriders. I do their accounts and hold my breath. All the while, the police are investigating Jesse's death – they get nowhere. They never ask me a damn thing. The local paper covers it for weeks but then the whole story just slips from view.

I start to unravel anyway.

There are too many questions left hanging.

I don't feel like I've got away with anything.

And Sock is dead now too. That spooks me. They found him hanging from a tree, not far from where I left him that day at the drive-in. He'd stripped himself naked and used his belt. There was a rumour going round that he'd rammed the handle of a shovel up his arse before stringing himself up. I don't know what that's about. Did the Riders do it? Someone told me once that suicidal people do weird shit like that before they kill themselves but I don't know.

The bikie clubhouse, the place they called Hell, isn't as bad as I expected. Their books are the real nightmare. They need someone like me; Dennis wasn't much of a bookkeeper. The Riders treat me with a degree of civility. They call me Lucky – like some sick reminder – but no one gets in my face. And of all places, Hell has air-conditioning. The humidity comes up late in October and steams Gatton raw, while I sit in the cool and look at numbers on a page.

They have me set up in an office off the main pool room. The tall guy in the cowboy hat – his name is Davis, as it turns out – gives me a desk and stationery. There is no computer. 'Can't burn a computer real quick,' says Davis. He is in charge of the Gatton branch of the club. The other one, Murph – the one who killed Dennis and Hatch – he is a rung above. Murph was only out for the night to get things in order. That is a relief, of sorts. And relief is in short supply.

I was an ex-drug dealer.

My best friend was a murderer and predator.

I let Iris down.

I nearly got us both killed.

I stood by and watched other people get killed.

These were real crimes.

It isn't like in the movies. It hasn't just resolved itself after a bunch of death and mayhem. I don't know where I stand with any of it.

Am I guilty?

Am I innocent?

I feel a lifetime opening up between those two things. A blank nothingness where I will never be a good person ever again, where I will never deserve a nice gesture or a kind moment. There are just too many dead people around. Too many abused women. Too much addiction, history, madness. Too much Jesse and Ray. Too much of everything and not enough energy to start sorting through it. As the days pass, I seem to sway between intense fear of death – that once I am done with the Doomriders' books, they'll be done with me – and days where I see my own death in intricate detail and welcome its arrival.

The pressure is getting to me. The uncertainty of it all was scrambling my mind.

I smoke every day, trying to stay calm.

I hit the goon bag.

I spiral.

Am I going to die too, with something up my arse like Sock?

Will the Doomriders hurt Iris after I'm gone?

Will the cops come in the night?

I take all of those questions – all etched in blood and violence and horror – and I try to seal them shut inside that black duffle bag of Jesse's money I still have stashed away. I put all that confusion and panic out there in the bush, under the ground, and try to concentrate on waking up every morning and staying as mashed as possible.

As I go, I repeat the same fucked up mantra:

Just keep breathing.

Sit on the money.

I have fever dreams where I open the black duffle bag and it was full of red raw human organs.

But I keep waking up.

There is more. During those final weeks of semester, things are just as upside down at home inside my caravan. Iris came round every night. After the incident, we fall into a malaise of microwaved pizza and hot-chip sandwiches, cassette tapes turning in the stereo. Our faces heal together. We have our anxiety attacks and nightmares together. Iris has it worse than me: she was tied up in that caravan with Dennis and Hatch for hours. But we are both still scared it isn't over.

So Iris stays close. She goes sober. That's how she deals with it, or what I think *it* is. She sleeps in my bed, showers in the park's communal showers, brings clothes and make-up round. She doesn't use her special chair anymore. In fact, she tossed it outside and now uses the closet space to store an empty suitcase. She has started putting on weight.

As the nights together wear on and we lay side by side in our sweated-through underwear, we keep quiet. We don't talk about what happened. What can we say, anyhow? And I can feel the silence taking us somewhere.

Eventually we come to do more than sleep side by side. We are both looking to feel something, *anything* other than the heat, and we find it in fucking. It works – it shuts me down. I blank out for hours at a time. We aren't on ecstasy this time. We barrel into it and I see the old Iris disappear. The girl from the neighbourhood. The girl from Beenleigh State High. The family friend. *My* friend. She is now the ghost of that person. A compilation of ghosts. As I run my hands over her wet skin, it erases things. It is like I never knew her, or myself, and in a sense that is true, isn't it?

My cashflow dries up, like I always feared it would. I let it go. The whole thing scares me now. Craig ends up taking over my customer base. The Riders need an in with the students and I hook them up. They end up expanding the business. Craig is first to market with a new one-stop service in Gatton: pills, space cake, weed and pizza. He delivers, driving around town in his van. He looks set to make more money than any of us in the old crew combined. I watch his business take shape in the backroom of Hell. Craig has his own code in the ledger.

The Riders have sorted me out with a private stash of weed and it is enough to split with my landlord Graham so I get to stay in the caravan park. The rest, I have to manage myself.

Including my parents...

I call home from a payphone.

My mother answers. She asks how school is.

I failed everything. Every subject.

I say, 'Put Dad on.'

Mum and I haven't spoken much since. It feels good.

Dad fumbles with the receiver. 'Hello?'

'It's me.'

'Oh, Nate. How's things? I've been worried.'

I don't answer. Instead, I burst out crying, just howling into the phone as I stand there by the side of the road, in the same phone box where all this started, the one by the highway caked in dust. The fucking sun still beaming down. Dad doesn't know any of this. He thinks I am crying because I'm weeks late with the side-money for that sixty-year mortgage of theirs. But I'm crying because hearing his voice cuts straight through me, straight to the core:

Jesse.

Ray.

Me.

We all hurt people.

We all asked for this.

This fucking horror.

This carnage swirling around.

Jesse was my best friend and I didn't even know him. Ray was my brother and I didn't even know him.

Two killers. Two predators. Two cowards. Two –

I did nothing.

Worse, with Jesse, I destroyed the evidence. I cleaned up after him. All for my own ends.

All for money.

All this death unleashed.

Dennis with the gushing hole in his head.

Hatch wimpering.
Sock...
The look in his eyes as I'm pissing on him.
And Maya...
I can't even force my mind back there.
It's like I buried her again.
All for money.
It was all for this money buried in a hole.
'You there, Nate? *Nate?*'
I look at the receiver in my hand.

There's a dark sliver that runs through some of us. Something unknown. I see that now. It's not in my dad. Mum maybe, but not Dad. And because of this, Dad starts pleading with me on the phone. He's begging me to forgive myself. 'We'll sort this mess out, Nate. Our money problems are not *your* problem. Your mother and I will find a way through this, we will. I promise.'

We're all the same, my brothers and I.

Fraternity.

Of a kind.

The guilt and anxiety push me in weird directions. About once a week, I drive past the house in Hickey Street where Maya Kibby used to live. I park around the corner by some brush near the rail line and from there I can watch the place in dark seclusion. The Kibby house is a little low-set brick place, a lot of glass in front. Her family are in the habit of leaving the blinds open. Maya had two little sisters. Her parents – a greying pitbull of a man and a Greek woman with dark eyes – they sit in front of the television and eat alone at the dinner table. In the long summer dusk, the little girls, the sisters, play in their nightgowns out on the street.

It gets to be a habit. I knew who killed Maya, their daughter, their sister. So I sat in the car and drink XXXX Gold and watch them, sometimes willing myself to go over and knock on their door, sometimes silently outraged – vividly angry – that they are getting on with their lives while I sit outside, waiting, with the truth sitting in my gut like rotten food.

When I am done staring, I drive home the same way, always the same way, snaking through a series of back streets to avoid police breath-testing. Half-drunk, that drive becomes a ritual, a pulse of something along a circuit board. *Why aren't you doing anything?* Winding its way back through the town, back to my home, back to my caravan and to my bed and Iris.

I'm at lunch. I'm back in the student refectory with the summer boarders. I've got my Maccas money but I still sneak in there and save myself five dollars when I feel like it. I see some people I know.

Donna and Spencer come by and say hi. They stand there and watch me eat my stolen spaghetti bolognaise and fill me in on their trip away together. *And then we hired this totally cute minivan and drove down the coast, oh my god, we didn't even get out of the car in Nimbin before someone tried to hook us up and...* I nod and sip at my apple juice and try to look interested. I'm not. I stare out across the room and the conversations blend together, becoming one low murmur.

That afternoon, my car idles and the engine shakes, desperate to stop. I look across at the Kibby family house and watch the two sisters running on the sidewalk outside. I crack open a beer and take a long gulp. Then suddenly, out through the windscreen, the two girls are watching me. They're standing in the road near the car with iridescent purple hula hoops around their ankles and they're staring. One of them points. I start the car and reverse hard, almost clipping a man standing behind me. He's wearing a blue shirt. I peel up the street.

The whole world spins off axis until I finish the six-pack. I spend an hour pacing up and down the caravan listening to 'Meantime' by Helmet. I have wine and I start on that. I have weed and I take a monstrous toke into my lungs. I take my shirt off. 'Come and get me, then,' I scream into the night for everyone to hear, but no one comes.

I jolt awake in the car. Dark out. Middle of the night. I'm parked in a street, houses all around me. I should not be driving. I have no idea how I got here. I look around. I'm back on Hickey Street, the train line running up the side. The Kibby house is half a block up. I wind down the window and warm air drifts in on the breeze. The street is still.

Raaaaar!

Something loud in the window. I holler and try to scramble over to the passenger seat with my seat belt still fastened. The belt locks and I glance over as I'm unclipping it: Maya Kibby's face lit up like a ghost in the window. She smiles and disappears.

I'm losing my mind.

'What the fuck?'

I look in the rear-view and see flashing light. Someone laughs back there, a giggle. Through the raw terror I start to feel what's really happening.

The back doors of the car jerk open and two small figures crawl up onto the rear bench. Two little girls. They both have flashlights and in unison they shine them under their faces.

Two Maya Kibbys.

The relief is so great I almost laugh.

'We've been waiting for you to come back,' says one of the Kibby sisters. 'Haven't we?'

The one on the left gives an exaggerated nod.

'What are you two doing out so late?' I say.

'We snuck out.'

I notice that they're both in little loose-fitting nighties and their feet are filthy. The younger one has a dummy hanging around her neck, tied in place with a piece of shoelace.

'You guys have to go back to bed.'

'Nuh-uh,' says the younger one.

'We've seen you watching us,' says the other one. 'They told us to keep an eye out for you, so we've been on the lookout.' She says this in a sing-song cadence, different words elongated and melodic. It's a game.

'Looking for me?'

'Are you drunk? You smell like our neighbour.'

I turn back to the wheel.

'I'm pretty drunk,' I say.

'My mummy says –'

'Girls, you've got to go back inside.'

The older one shuffles forward and drapes an arm over the headrest. She whispers, 'Are you trying to kill us?'

'*What?* Okay, you both need to… No, no darling, I'm not going to hurt anyone. I… I knew your sister. That's all.'

'May-ya,' says the little one.

'That's right.'

'She died,' says the older one.

'I know. I'm sorry.'

The girls sit still for a moment. I reach out and touch the keys in the ignition, trying to run down ways to get them out of the car.

'A boy killed her,' says the older one. 'A boy just like you, that's what Mummy said.'

'Not like me.'

'Good.' And she turns to her sister and says, 'See, I told you.'

'Good,' says the other one.

'I'm really happy now,' says the older girl.

'Happy,' echoes the other one.

'Our neighbour sent the bad boy away. We didn't want you to go away too. We like you.'

'What?'

The older one says, 'You can stay if you're a good boy but if you're a bad boy, our neighbour will come and send you away too.'

'Away where?'

'Into the ground,' says the girl.

'Bye-bye,' says her sister. 'Bye-bye.'

The other one says it too: 'Bye-bye, bye-bye.'

They slip back out of the car and start to run back to the house. I'm so stunned I can't move. When they're halfway back across the road, I get out and run after them, catching the older one by the arm.

'Wait, wait. Which neighbour?'

She's laughing, squirming away from me, flashing the light on and off.

'Alex,' she says.

'Which house?'

She shines the beam of the flashlight around onto a house, a two-storey white fibro bungalow on stilts, no garden or fence. I sprint back to the car and start the engine. *Easy, drive slow.* I put the indicator on and creep up Hickey Street and as I pass the house the little girl showed me, I stop breathing. There's a police car parked in the drive.

I should have known. A local girl dies and the police do nothing. A student dies and the police do nothing. Two bikies go missing and the police do nothing. Murder, suicide, pornography, drug running, gangs and a university. Nothing. No course of action. They should have been all over every part of my life this last year but they weren't. They never came for me.

It's 10:40 a.m.

I haven't slept.

It doesn't make sense. I can't join up all the details. There's no linear story that explains the things I know, all the things I've seen and done. I've gone too far with my erasure.

But it makes sense somewhere else, though:

In my gut.

Both houses are deserted, the Kibby place and the house across the road. I'm on foot, it's nearly midday and everyone can see me walking the streets. I have a sports bag with me and inside the sports bag is a bunch of impulses:

My gun, wrapped in a towel. The same piece Murph used on Hatch. Davis insisted I keep it, *for protection*.

I also have:

My hammer.

A pair of winter gloves.

A plastic mask. *Robocop*. From last year's Bachelor of Business Halloween party.

Baby wipes.

A roll of wire.

A roll of gaffer tape.

A dictaphone I tape lectures with.

A book.

I'm not sure why I have this exact list of things. I threw the bag together in a hurry. I planned to just bring the empty bag but once I had it open on the bed, I figured I may as well take the gun – *for protection* – and the rest followed. I'm regretting it now as the weight of the bag cuts into my shoulder.

I walk over to the Kibby's neighbour's house, the one the girl pointed out. The police car is gone. I open the screen and knock, fairly certain that no one is home.

I'm right. No answer.

I try the door. It's locked.

I dart around the house, climb the rear stairs and try that door. Unlocked. An enclosed verandah: work boots on the ragged carpet, an axe, a collection of auto parts. There's an internal door there and it's locked but it comes open with the first kick.

Inside, the house is small. I can hear from one far wall to the other.

I scan around:

An abandoned cup of tea.

Fresh toast in the bin.

An empty milk bottle by the fridge.

Dust motes in the air.

The eerie stillness of another person's life.

There are two rooms off the main kitchen and dining area. I'm definitely dealing with a single man. I can tell before I open the closet. He sleeps in one room and uses the other as some sort of study. I case the bedroom first, making a mess, ripping out anything I can get my hands on. He's living lean. A few outfits, all folded. Pressed police uniforms on hangers. One spare set of dress shoes. There's a box of late '80s *Penthouse* magazines in the back of the closet and disassembled exercise weights on the floor. That's it.

In the study there's a computer but it's password-protected. He has a bunch of rugby stuff on the walls, jerseys and prizes. The closet in there is empty.

There's nothing suspect about any of it.

I sit in his office chair and look at the walls.

Then I go out to the living room and pry open the venetian blinds and stare across the street. He can see every part of the Kibby house from here. Even parts of the back yard are visible.

I feel sick.

I check his fridge and it's almost empty. He has a six-pack of Coke cans and a box of cold chips from Red Rooster. I pass on both. Instead, I go to the living room and lay my stuff out on the floor, resting the gun and the mask on the cushion beside me. I look at the door and wait. After a while, I take the book out of my bag. *Innovation and Entrepreneurship* by Peter F. Drucker. I open it up.

He comes an hour after dark and suspects nothing. His car stereo plays loudly as he pulls up and dies immediately as he kills the engine. I hear the mailbox open and close. Then the stairs creak and the lock turns. I see him as he steps in: this tall man with short cropped hair in a police uniform. *That uniform.* He carries a box – a carton of beer – under one arm and a bag of groceries under the other. He does not check the room before he closes the door behind him. He does not see me standing there with the shotgun at shoulder level, staring down the barrel at him through a plastic *Robocop* mask.

'Don't. Fucking. Move,' I hiss.

The groceries drop but not the beer.

He goes to run. It's just two steps.

'Ah! *WhatdidIsay!* What did I fucking say?'

He stops.

'Come over here. Sit down. No, keep holding onto the beer. Just sit on that. No, that.'

He sits on a footstool I've set out and places the beer carton on his lap. He's so big it looks ridiculous, like a giant teetering on a miniature chair. Yet his bulk has a softness to it. His shoulders are slumped and he's getting wide around the waist. His eyes have a tired watery quality to them and his skin is oily; it glistens, even in the low light.

'What's your name?' I say.

'Alex.'

'Alex what?'

'Alex Sennett.'

It sounds familiar.

I remember his gun and step left. It's there, holstered to his belt.

'Throw that over there. Do it slow.'

Alex takes it out. The carton of beer teeters on his knees.

'It's not a good idea,' he says.

'What?'

'Throwing it. It could discharge... if I throw it.'

I don't know what he's playing at but he looks serious.

'Put it on the carpet and nudge it away with your foot.'

'Okay.'

He pushes it my way. I take a split second to look down, which is hard with the mask on, and then I put my foot beside the gun, gently sweeping it away from him.

'You mind if I open this?' he says.

'You want a beer?'

'Are you here to kill me?'

'No,' I say, regretting it instantly.

'Then I'm going to have a beer.'

I nod.

'You want one?'

'I'm good.'

He turns the beer carton up and opens it, slipping a VB out. Alex takes a long drink before draping both his arms back over the carton. I take a good look at him.

He's the cop who stopped me in Jesse's street, back in September. The one who stuck his head in the car.

'What do you want?' he says. 'Who are you?'

'I'm fucking Robocop. Don't ask me who I am, Jesus. I want to talk to you about Jesse Koerstz.'

'Oh yeah? Who's that, then?'

'He's the guy that you killed over in Goltz Street last year. Ringing any bells?'

'What do you care?'

'What? What do I –'

'Your boys know you're here?'

'Who? I don't…'

He narrows his eyes. 'You know who I reckon you are? My guess is you're his mate from the caravan park, the one who's stitched up with the Doomriders now. You should be careful with that. They're protecting you and they're a pretty good lot, good to their word and all, but there's plenty of other people who would be real interested in what you've seen. *Real* interested. A lot of people, people who aren't so good to their word.' When he's done he takes another long pull on the stubbie, draining it.

I take a step closer. I put the barrel closer. 'So you killed him, then?'

He looks up at me. 'Yeah. Yeah, I did.' The way he says it isn't steady or confident. He immediately looks away.

There's a pause. A breeze rattles the blinds in the other room.

'Why?' I'm still standing over him with the gun. 'How did you even know Jesse?'

'I didn't know him... I knew her.'

'Maya?'

'Yeah.'

'And?'

'You sure you don't want a beer? I'm gonna have another. It's all I fucking do since all this happened. You may as well sit down.'

'I'm all right,' I say.

'Well, you're scaring me so if it's all the same...'

'Start at the beginning.'

Alex Sennett rubs at his face and smiles a frustrated smile. 'Why?'

'Because I want to know.'

'The best thing you can do right now is to take your gun and your mask and all this and get out of here. Just go home and leave town. Don't tell the Riders, don't tell the uni, just go and –'

He stops because the gun is touching him now.

He closes his eyes.

'No,' I say. 'Time to put this to bed.'

'Okay, okay, shit. Just...'

'Hurry up.'

Alex Sennett breathes out. 'I thought I was going to the grave with this. But if you want to...' He looks at his hands and shakes his head. 'If you want to share this load with me, be my guest.'

Alex says he knew Maya since the day she was born, had lived across the road from the family all that time. He was ten years older but it didn't matter. They were friends from the moment she could talk. Maya Kibby was a good kid: funny, quiet, kind to her parents and kind to his. She was a dreamer, though, and, 'You know, probably the only person I ever met who might have gotten those dreams too. That's how it felt with her.' And then she wasn't any of those things. Overnight, she was a news article. A memorial. Just parts of a body, buried in a ditch out in the scrub, dug up by a dog.

'You know, my parents... they're both dead. It was just me and them. I haven't got any brothers or sisters. Dad got cancer. I thought... Oh god, I thought he'd die at work, on the job, he was a cop too. Not like me. He was a better cop than me. But I thought he'd just drop dead out on patrol. But no, he died real slow, in and out of hospital for months, years, and he took my mother with him. She didn't last much more than a year without him. And so here I am, on my own all of a sudden at, fuck, twenty-two, not much older than you are now. You know who looked after me? They did,' and he nods in the direction of their house. 'Maya's mum cooked for me for months, sent her across with food. And you know, as bad as it was, it wasn't wrong, what happened with Mum and Dad. That's life. I've learned that now, seen it plenty more on the job, plenty of old dead people. People die. People get cancer all the time. It happens every day. But what happened to Maya, that...'

I'm sitting down now.

'Jesse?' I say.

He nods.

'It was wrong,' he says.

He takes out another beer out and uncaps it.

Maya had a hidey-hole underneath the tank stand behind the house. Her little sisters knew about it. After she went missing, the sisters went through her stuff and found a bag of weed, a box of condoms, a pile of cash and a notebook. The notebook had poems, lists, phone numbers. One name appeared over and over: Hatch.

'Hatch and Maya had been fooling around, off and on,' says Alex. 'No one knew about it. He was a bit older than her but they went to the same school up here. He was actually not a bad kid, back in the day, till the Riders got their hooks in him. I don't know what she saw in him now that he was all grown up.' He stops. 'Did you know her? I guess it's not the sort of thing you see in people you grow up with, especially little girls.'

Iris.

He burps and punches his fist into his solar plexus, trying to dislodge the air.

'And?' I say.

'That's where the whole thing gets a bit complicated.' He punches his chest again. 'Jesus. It's good, I suppose.'

'What is?'

'The complication.'

'Is it?'

'It's why neither of us are in prison.'

Dennis and Hatch were moving pills into the Lockyer Valley without permission from the higher-ups in the Doomriders. Worse still, the supply chain was a nightmare. The pills came from Brisbane, from a group of guys in the Brisbane police who were grafting them out of various raids down there, raids that included takedowns of the Brisbane branch of the Doomriders. The stuff was way too hot to move in the city, so the bent coppers down there sent the gear out into the regions and the regions were trying all sorts of ways and means to off-load it.

'My senior sergeant is married to Hatch's aunt. He hooked them up with that stuff from Brisbane and we were all set up for a little payday. I didn't think much of it, to be honest. I didn't even really know what ecstasy was. I don't go in for that sort of thing. So we hooked up Hatch and he and Dennis went off and started moving the gear around town. He puts the feelers out for someone to rep the student side of things on campus and Maya introduced them.'

'Jesse?'

'Yeah.'

'How'd she know Jesse? I can't work it out.'

'The *directors*, that's what she called them in the diary,' says Alex. 'She doesn't use their names but I figure you know who we're talking about. She wanted to be in movies. She was saving up to go to acting school in the city. She needed something... a show-something, like a tape of her acting.'

Sock. He's local. Same age. He knows her from around town. He's making movies. He can make a showreel. And she needs money, which brings in Jesse and his business.

I say, 'And then what?'

'I went round there, after she died?'

'Why? How'd you put that together.'

He looks at me, right into my face. 'A tape. Someone put a tape in my mailbox. It showed...' He pushes out a long slow breath. His eyes are glistening.

'Yeah,' I say.

'Oh, so you've seen it?'

'Not like that. I didn't know what they were up to.'

He breathes out. 'I was going to arrest him but... I lost it, as soon as I saw him. I just... I fucked everything up. I waited for him to come home and I was so fucking angry, and I dunno, crazy, but I started pounding on him the moment he came inside. I don't really remember it. I remember starting to choke him, like grabbing him and pushing him into a corner but I don't remember anything else... I...'

And suddenly Alex is weeping. He's staring at his hands, streams of tears rolling out of his eyes. 'I...' He looks like he might come off the stool; the carton wobbles on his knees. 'I... Now we can't finish anything,' he sobs. 'I sit here and... that's the worst part. I killed that kid and he was the only... I've got to live with it but... I just... Her family, they'll... What am I supposed to do? I can't do anything. I do *anything* – I go to jail or to a shallow grave with that bikie gang. *What* am I supposed to do? *What?*'

I put the gun down.

'You're okay,' I say. 'I know how you feel.'

'I don't even know why he did it. Do you?'

I shake my head. 'No. I don't think he did it for a reason.'

Alex coughs and wipes his nose.

I take off the mask and I tell him the truth.

'You did the right thing.'

And then I tell him everything else I've learned about Jesse before I show him the dictaphone.

I wake up.

Iris is sitting on the end of the bed. The air is cool for a change, dawn's approaching.

'What did you do with the tapes?' she says.

'What tapes?'

'Jesse's videotapes. Let's just talk. Can we do that?'

'I got rid of them.'

'They're gone?'

'Yeah. I burned them.'

She looks over. She seems impressed. 'Good.'

'Do you know who killed him?'

Iris exhales. She doesn't know about my trip over to Alex Sennett's house two nights ago. Iris is a mess. Straight but barely there half the time now. She's just dazed, somehow. She keeps throwing up.

'Maybe,' she says. 'What are you going to do?'

'I don't know. What are you going to do?'

'Nothing. Jesse wasn't a very good person, was he?'

'No.'

'I don't think I even really liked him, that's the funny thing. It was all so... *transactional* with him. Always business. We were his best friends, you and I, but... did you actually like him? Like deep down?'

'I don't know.'

I get up and put the jug on.

'Do you know what I think?' she says. 'I think it was *you* he wanted. I think he was into guys, into dick. I think that's where all this bullshit starts. It's one explanation, anyhow. It's almost funny because it's what I wanted too. We both wanted the same person, the same guy. We wanted you. And you, *you* walked around thinking the world was against you, that everyone hated your guts, that you were alone. But you were never alone.'

I lie down on the lino beside the sink. I continue to listen but I don't want to.

'I didn't kill him, Nate. I didn't.'

'Okay.'

I stare at the ceiling. 'Who killed him, then?' It's a dare.

'He killed himself.'

'Just like Sock.'

'Close enough.'

Iris comes over and straddles me. She hikes up her skirt up. She's dry so she spits into her hand and wipes my cock down, sliding over me. It takes a while for it to work but when it's done she lies on my chest and heaves in deep breaths. She says there's more but she can't talk about it.

We lie like that for a long time.

Then, like a ghost in the dark, she says:

'Do you know where his money is?'

This is the big lesson I learned at university: forgetting is a type of debt. Last year, I was living a precarious life, surveying the world as if I'd forgotten that people can change as quickly as markets; that new sides of situations can appear without contingency; that things aren't always as they seem. I somehow forgot that dark incentives sit beneath the surface of people. And I know it's crazy – so, so crazy – in light of what I've lived through with my brother and my mother. But I think that might be it: I was naive by design. I wanted things to be straightforward for once, like before Ray died. I wanted to win. And I wanted money. What I really wanted was supply and demand without moral complication, and that never happens. There's *always* a price where those two things intersect. There's always a cost when history meets the present.

And when:

Iris's belly swells and bulges in the new year, it's the baby inside her, finally revealing itself. She doesn't change otherwise. She finds another place to live, a caravan of her own, by the caravan park's pool. Later, in her last trimester, I dig up Jesse's money and give her half. I ask her – just once – if the baby is mine and she says, 'I doubt it.' As I'm walking back to my van she calls out: 'Have you ever held a baby in your arms? It gives you something, Nate. You'll see.'

And when:

I finally finish my time with the Doomriders and they gave me a beating – and a short stay in Toowoomba hospital – just to remind me where we stand and how things *could* go.

And when:

I start paying down the mortgage on my family home – in bigger, faster sums to save the place – and the look on Dad's face is one I've seen before. He doesn't ask but a part of him knows where my money's coming from. Not the details. Just that it's from somewhere bad, somewhere Ray has been. I think he can see it in my eyes. Across the table, my mother stirs her coffee and changes the subject.

And when:

I see Alex Sennett in the dairy aisle of Coles and he says hello, with his red plastic shopping basket in hand. He asks about my studies. I tell him I'm finished and it's the truth. I've dropped out of my business degree. I don't want to learn any more. We all are who we are now. It's an early graduation of sorts.

And finally when:

I carry on.

But each Friday night I let myself slip a little. I pack that bong and hit play on the cassette player and the guitars wail and the voices screech and the van shudders. Bong smoke sits like a storm cloud under the low ceiling, but I spark that cone again and again. I drag deep and the night roars. Through it, I hear the buzzing sound of my pager. *Iris.* I grab the keys to my car and laugh. My heart's racing but I stop at the door to my van and slowly exhale into the night air. This is the last of it coming out now, that last little bit of who I was, before I arrived at this final moment.

ACKNOWLEDGEMENTS

I'd like to thank David and Beryl Rogers, Lee Earle, Hercules Kollias, Benjamin Law, DP, Caro Cooper, Andrew Nette, J. David Osborne, Liam José, David Honeybone, Gabriella West, Benjamin Thompson, Amy Vuleta, Angela Meyer, Emma Viskic, David Whish-Wilson, Tracy O'Shaughnessy, Gary Kemble, Nicola Williams, Adrian McKinty and Clive Hebard. Apologies to the people of Gatton. Special thanks to Clare Chippendale who hated this novel but remains a constant source of inspiration and encouragement. I love you, Clare.

Ghost Girls by Cath Ferla

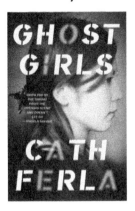

**A student leaps to her death.
Was the girl who she said she was?**

Unable to resist the investigative instincts that run in her blood, Sophie Sandilands finds herself unravelling a sinister operation that is trawling the foreign student market for its victims. But as she works on tracking down the criminals, it becomes clear that someone knows about the ghosts in her own past. Is there anyone left that Sophie can trust?

Ghost Girls richly evokes the sights, smells, tastes and sounds of Sydney's Chinatown, and imagines dark exploitative demands behind closed suburban doors.

> 'Ferla has a gift for description and brings alive the small restaurants and dark corners of Sydney frequented mainly by foreign students. The characters are convincing and interesting and the plot, involving student visa fraud and the sex trade, up-to-date and chilling.' – *Sydney Morning Herald*

> 'A riveting murder mystery about international students, violence, exploitation, sinister operatives in the underground sex world and identity fraud.' – *Australian Financial Review*

Paperback	9781760406967
Epub	9781760401184
Kindle	9781760401191

Resurrection Bay by Emma Viskic

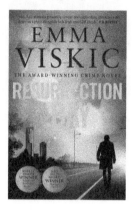

Caleb Zelic, profoundly deaf since early childhood, has always lived on the outside – watching, picking up tell-tale signs people hide in a smile, a cough, a kiss. When a childhood friend is murdered, a sense of guilt and a determination to prove his own innocence sends Caleb on a hunt for the killer. But he can't do it alone. Caleb and his troubled friend Frankie, an ex-cop, start with one clue: Scott, the last word the murder victim texted to Caleb. But Scott is always one step ahead. As he delves deeper into the investigation Caleb uncovers unwelcome truths about his murdered friend – and himself.

'A rattling plot-driven thriller that is not for the faint-hearted … never takes a predictable turn.' – *The Age*

'A highly enjoyable debut.' – *The Daily Telegraph*

'Viskic's characterisation, dialogue and plotting are on par with some of the heavyweights of crime writing.' – *Sydney Morning Herald*

'An outstanding debut novel.' – *Newtown Review of Books*

'Intricately plotted.' – *Artshub*

'You will not forget this story, you will not forget this cast of characters.' – *Reading, Writing And Riesling*

'Viskic has balanced first class character development with palpable violence and suspense' – *Booklover Book Reviews*

Paperback	9781760406943
Epub	9781760069797
Kindle	9781760069803

And Fire Came Down by Emma Viskic

Deaf since early childhood, Caleb Zelic is used to meeting life head-on. Now, he's struggling just to get through the day. His best mate is dead, his ex-wife, Kat, is avoiding him, and nightmares haunt his waking hours.

But when a young woman is killed, after pleading for his help in sign language, Caleb is determined to find out who she was. The trail leads Caleb back to his hometown, Resurrection Bay. The town is on bushfire alert, and simmering with racial tensions. As Caleb delves deeper, he uncovers secrets that could ruin any chance of reuniting with Kat, and even threaten his life. Driven by his own demons, he pushes on. But who is he willing to sacrifice along the way?

Emma Viskic's critically acclaimed debut novel that featured Caleb Zelik, *Resurrection Bay*, won the 2016 Ned Kelly Award for Best First Fiction, as well as an unprecedented three Davitt Awards: Best Adult Novel, Best Debut, and Readers' Choice. *Resurrection Bay* was also iBooks Australia's Crime Novel of the Year in 2015.

Paperback 9781760402945
Epub 9781760402983
Kindle 9781760402990

Skin Deep by Gary Kemble

Shortlisted for the Ned Kelly Award for Best First Fiction

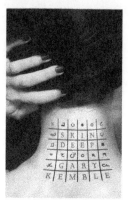

When washed-up journalist Harry Hendrick wakes with a hangover and a strange symbol tattooed on his neck, he shrugs it off as a bad night out.

When more tattoos appear — accompanied by visions of war-torn Afghanistan, bikies, boat people, murder, bar fights and a mysterious woman — he begins to dig a little deeper.

There's a federal election looming, with pundits tipping a landslide win for opposition leader Andrew Cardinal. Harry knows there's a link between these disturbing visions and Cardinal's shadowy past, and is compelled to right wrongs, one way or another.

> 'With an intense and immediate sense of place, a cracking pace and a great everyman hero, *Skin Deep* is by turns thrilling and haunting, and will keep readers glued to the page.' – *Angela Slatter*

> 'Not many ghost stories have this kind of immediacy, or tactility. No strange frissons or fleeting shadows here! It's all blood, drained batteries and murderous rage, stinking of bourbon in the subtropical humidity.' – *Tabula Rasa*

> '*Skin Deep* is a fine debut for both Kemble and Echo, which offers more than a passing nod to John Birmingham and Stephen King.' – *Books + Publishing*

Paperback 9781760406950
Epub 9781760069018
Kindle 9781760069025

Bad Blood by Gary Kemble

Freelance journalist Harry Hendrick is beginning to realise that you're only as good as your last exclusive, and buzz doesn't pay the bills, when he's blackmailed by the police into investigating a series of bizarre suicides.

Those investigations lead him into the web of Mistress Hel, who plies her dark arts from her luxurious suburban lair. With continuing challenges in his personal and professional life, can Harry resist her seductive power? Or the thrill of danger itself?

The second in the thrilling, genre-bending Harry Hendrick series by Gary Kemble.

> 'With grime on the surface and a fat seam of weird menacing below, Gary Kemble has crafted a thriller that pulls you in and keeps its cuffs on you to the last page.' – *Nick Earls*

Paperback	9781760406974
Epub	9781760402969
Kindle	9781760402976

Fatal Crossing by Lone Theils

When a picture of two Danish girls who disappeared in a boat bound for England in 1985 surfaces in an old suitcase, journalist Nora Sand's professional curiosity is immediately awakened.

Before she knows it, she is mixed up in a case of a serial killer serving a life sentence in a notorious prison. The quest to discover the truth about the missing girls may be more dangerous than she had ever imagined...

'A fast-paced and skillfully plotted thriller.' – *Barry Forshaw*

'*Fatal Crossing* creeps up on you, and before you know it, you are hooked.' – *Stefan Arnhem*, author of *The Ninth Grave*

'A candidate for the best crime novel of the year.' – *Krimi-Cirklin*

Paperback	9781760406530
Epub	9781760406547
Kindle	9781760406554